Nikola Tesla

EXPERIMENTS

WITH

ALTERNATE CURRENTS

OF

HIGH POTENTIAL AND HIGH FREQUENCY

EXPERIMENTS

WITH

ALTERNATE CURRENTS

OF

HIGH POTENTIAL AND HIGH FREQUENCY

BY

NIKOLA TESLA.

A LECTURE

DELIVERED BEFORE THE

INSTITUTION OF ELECTRICAL ENGINEERS, LONDON

With a portrait and Biographical Sketch of the Author.

KALPAZ

ISBN: 978-93-5128-527-4

First Published in 1892
Indian Reprint in 2017

Published by

Kalpaz Publications
C-30, Satyawati Nagar,
Delhi – 110052
E-mail: kalpaz@hotmail.com
Website: kalpazpublications.com
Ph.: +91-9212142040

Cataloging in Publication Data—DK
Courtesy: D.K. Agencies (P) Ltd. <docinfo@dkagencies.com>

Tesla, Nikola, 1856-1943, author.
Experiments with alternate currents of high potential and high frequency : a lecture delivered before the Institution of Electrical Engineers, London : with a portrait and biographical sketch of the author / by Nikola Tesla.
pages cm
Reprint. Originally published: New York : The W.J. Johnston Company Ltd, 1892.
ISBN 9789351285274

1. Electric currents, Alternating. 2. Electric discharges. 3. Telegraph, Wireless. I. Title.

QC641.T47 2017 DDC 537.6 23

Biographical Sketch of Nikola Tesla

While a large portion of the European family has been surging westward during the last three or four hundred years, 'Settling the vast continents of America, another, but smaller, portion has been doing frontier work in the Old World, protecting the rear by beating back the "unspeakable Turk" and reclaiming gradually the fair lands that endure the curse of Mohammedan rule. For a long time the Slav people — who, after the battle of Kosovopjolje, in which the Turks defeated the Servians, retired to the confines of the present Montenegro, Dalmatia, Herzegovina and Bosnia, and "Borderland" of Austria — knew what it was to deal, as our Western pioneers did, with foes ceaselessly fretting against their frontier ; and the races of these countries, through their strenuous struggle against the armies of the Crescent, have developed notable qualities of bravery and sagacity, while maintaining a patriotism and independence unsurpassed in any other nation.

It was in this interesting border region, and from among these valiant Eastern folk, that Nikola Tesla was born in the year 1857, and the fact that he, today, finds himself in America and one of our foremost electricians, is striking evidence of the extraordinary attractiveness alike of electrical pursuits and of the country where electricity enjoys its widest application.

Mr. Tesla's native place was Smiljan, Lika, where his father was an eloquent clergyman of the Greek Church, in which, by the way, his family is still prominently represented. His mother enjoyed great fame throughout the country side for her skill and originality in needlework, and doubtless transmitted her ingenuity to Nikola; though it naturally took another and more masculine direction.

The boy was early put to his books, and upon his father's removal to Gospic he spent four years in the public school, and later, three years in the Real School, as it is called. His escapades were such as most quickwitted boys go through, although he varied the programme on one occasion by getting imprisoned in a remote mountain chapel rarely visited for service; and on another occasion by falling headlong into a huge kettle of boiling milk, just drawn from the paternal herds. A third curious episode was that connected with his efforts to fly when, attempting to navigate the air with the aid of an old umbrella, he had, as might be expected, a very bad fall, and was laid up for six weeks.

About this period he began to take delight in arithmetic and physics. One queer notion he had was to work out everything by three or the power of three. He was now sent to an aunt at Cartstatt, Croatia, to finish his studies in what is known as the Higher Real School. It was there that, coming from the rural fastnesses, he saw a steam engine for the first time with a pleasure that he remembers to this day. At Cartstatt he was so diligent as to compress the four years' course into three, and graduated in 1873. Returning home during an epidemic of cholera, he was stricken down by the disease and suffered so seriously from the consequences that his studies were interrupted for fully two years. But the time was not wasted, for he had become passionately fond of experimenting, and as much as his means and leisure permitted devoted his eneres to electrical study and investigation. Up to this period it had been his father's intention to make a priest of him, and the idea hung over the young physicist like a very sword of Damocles. Finally he prevailed upon his worthy but reluctant sire to send him to Gratz in Austria to finish his studies at the Polytechnic School, and to prepare for work as professor of mathematics and physics. At Gratz he saw and operated a Gramme machine for the first time, and was so struck with the objections to the use of commutators and brushes that he made up his mind there and then to remedy that defect in dynamo-electric machines. In the second year of his course he abandoned the intention of becoming a teacher and took up the engineering curriculum. After three years of absence he returned home, sadly, to see his father die ; but, having resolved to settle down in Austria, and recognizing the value of linguistic acquirements, he went to Prague and then to Buda-Pesth with the view of mastering the languages he deemed necessary. Up to this time he had never realized the enormous sacrifices that his parents had made in promoting his education, but he now began to feel the pinch and to grow unfamiliar with the image of Francis Joseph I. There was considerable lag between his dispatches and the corresponding remittance from home; and when the mathematical expression for the value of the lag assumed the shape of an eight laid flat on its back, Mr. Tesla became a very fair example of high thinking and plain living, but he made up his mind to the struggle and determined to go through depending solely on his own resources. Not desiring the fame of a faster, he cast about for a livelihood, and through the help of friends he secured a berth as assistant in the engineering department of the government telegraphs. The salary was five dollars a week. This brought him into direct contact with practical electrical work and ideas, but it is needless to say that his means did not admit of much experimenting. By the time he had extracted several hundred thousand square and cube roots for the public benefit, the limitations, financial and otherwise, of the position had become painfully apparent, and he concluded that the best thing to do was to make a valuable invention. He proceeded at once to make inventions, but their value was visible only to the eye of faith, and they brought no grist to the mill. Just at this time the telephone made its appearance in Hungary, and the success of that great invention determined his career, hopeless as the profession had thus far seemed to him. He associated himself at once with telephonic work, and made various telephonic inventions, including an operative repeater; but it did not take him long to discover that, being so remote from the scenes of electrical activity, he was apt to spend time on aims and results already reached by others, and to lose touch. Longing for new opportunities and anxious for the development of which he felt himself possible, if once he could place himself within the genial and direct influences of the gulf streams of electrical thought, he broke away from the ties 'and traditions of the past, and in 1881 made his way to Paris. Arriving in that city, the ardent young Likan obtained employment as an electrical engineer with one of the largest electric lighting companies. The next year he went to Strasburg to install a plant, and on returning to Paris sought to carry out a number of ideas that had now ripened into inventions. About this time, however, the remarkable progress of America in electrical industry attracted his attention, and once again staking everything on a single throw, he crossed the Atlantic.

Mr. Tesla buckled down to work as soon as he landed on these shores, put his best thought and skill into it, and soon saw openings for his talent. In a short while a proposition was made to him to start his own company, and, accepting the terms, he at once worked up a practical sys- tem of arc lighting, as well as a potential method of dynamo regulation, which in one form is now known as the "third brush regulation." He also devised a thermo-magnetic motor and other kindred devices, about which little was published, owing to legal complications. Early in 1887 the Tesla Electric Company of New York was formed. and not long after that Mr. Tesla produced his admirable and epoch-marking motors for multiphase alternating currents, in which, going back to his ideas of long ago, he evolved machines having neither commutator nor brushes. It will be remembered that about the time that Mr. Tesla brought out his motors, and read his thoughtful paper before the American Institute of Electrical Engineers, Professor Ferraris, in Europe, published his discovery of principles analogous to those ennunciated by Mr Tesla. There is no doubt, however, that Mr. Tesla was an independent inventor of this rotary field motor, for although anticipated in dates by Ferraris, he could not have known about Ferraris' work as it had not been published. Professor Ferraris stated himself, with becoming modesty, that he did not think Tesla could have known of his (Ferraris') experiments at that time, and adds that he thinks Tesla was an independent and original inventor of this principle. With such an acknowledgment from Ferraris there can be little doubt about Tesla's originality in this matter.

Mr Tesla's work in this field was wonderfully timely, and its worth was promptly appreciated in various quarters. The Tesla patents were acquired by the Westinghouse Electric Company, who undertook to develop his motor and to apply it to work of different kinds. Its use in mining, and its employment in printing, ventilation, etc., was described and illustrated in The Electrical World some years ago. The immense stimulus that the announcement of Mr. Tesla's work gave to the study of alternating current motors would, in itself, be enough to stamp him as a leader.

Mr. Tesla is only 35 years of age. He is tall and spare with a clean-cut, thin, refined face, and eyes that recall all the stories one has read of keenness of vision and phenomenal ability to see through things. He is an omnivorous reader, who never forgets; and he possesses the peculiar facility in languages that enables the least educated native of eastern Europe to talk and write in at least half a dozen tongues. A more congenial companion cannot be desired for the hours when one "pours out heart affluence in discursive talk," and when the conversation, dealing at first with things near at hand and next to us, reaches out and rises to the greater questions of life, duty and destiny.

In the year 1890 he severed his connection with the Westinghouse Company, since which time he has devoted him-self entirely to the study of alternating currents of high frequencies and very high potentials, with which study he is at present engaged. No comment is necessary on his interesting achievements in this field; the famous London lecture published in this volume is a proof in itself. His first lecture on his researches in this new branch of electricity, which he may be said to have created, was delivered before the American Institute of Electrical Engineers on May 20, 1891, and remains one of the most interesting papers read before that society. It will be found reprinted in full in The Electrical World, July 11, 1891. Its publication excited such interest abroad that he received numerous requests from English and French electrical engineers and scientists to repeat it in those countries, the result of which has been the interesting lecture published in this volume.

The present lecture presupposes a knowledge of the former, but it may be read and understood by any one even though he has not read the earlier one. It forms a sort of continuation of the latter, and includes chiefly the results of his researches since that time.

EXPERIMENTS

WITH

Alternate Currents of High Potential and High Frequency

I cannot find words to express how deeply I feel the honor of addressing some of the foremost thinkers of the present time, and so many able scientific men, engineers and electricians, of the country greatest in scientific achievements.

The results which I have the honor to present before such a gathering I cannot call my own. There are among you not a few who can lay better claim than myself on any feature of merit which this work may contain. I need not mention many names which are world-known—names of those among you who are recognized as the leaders in this enchanting science; but one, at least, I must mention—a name which could not be omitted in a demonstration of this kind. It is a name associated with the most beautiful invention ever made: it is Crookes!

When I was at college, a good time ago; I read, in a translation (for then I was not familiar with you magnificent language), the description of his experiments on radiant matter. I read it only once in my life—that time—yet every detail about that charming work I can remember this day. Few are the books, let me say, which can make such an impression upon the mind of a student.

But if, on the present occasion, I mention this name as one of many your institution can boast of, it is because I have more than one reason to do so. For what I have to tell you and to show you this evening concerns, in a large measure, that same vague world which Professor Crookes has so ably explored; and, more than this, when I trace back the mental process which led me to these advances—which even by myself cannot be considered trifling, since they are so appreciated by you—I believe that their real origin, that which started me to work in this direction, and brought me to them, after a long period of constant thought, was that fascinating little book which I read many years ago.

And now that I have made a feeble effort to express my homage and acknowledge my indebtedness to him and others among you, I will make a second effort, which I hope you will not find so feeble as the first, to entertain you.

Give me leave to introduce the subject in a few words.

A short time ago I had the honor to bring before our American Institute of Electrical Engineers* some results then arrived at by me in a novel line of work. I need not assure you that the many evidences which I have received that English scientific men and engineers were interested in this work have been for me a great reward and encouragement. I will not dwell upon the experiments already described, except with the view of completing, or more clearly expressing, some ideas advanced by me before, and also with the view of rendering the study here presented self-contained, and my remarks on the subject of this evening's lecture consistent.

This investigation, then, it goes without saying, deals with alternating currents, and, to be more precise, with alternating currents of high potential and high frequency. Just in how much a very high frequency is essential for the production of the results presented is a question which, even with my present experience, would embarrass me to answer. Some of the experiments may be performed with low frequencies; but very high frequencies are desirable, not only on account of the many effects secured by their use, but also as a convenient means of obtaining, in the induction apparatus employed, the high potentials, which in their turn are necessary to the demonstration of most of the experiments here contemplated.

Of the various branches of electrical investigation, perhaps the most interesting and immediately the most promising is that dealing with alternating currents. The progress in this branch of applied science has been so great in recent years that it justifies the most sanguine hopes. Hardly have we become familiar with one fact, when novel experiences are met with and new avenues of research are opened. Even at this hour possibilities not dreamed of before are, by the use of these currents, partly realized. As In nature all is ebb and tide, all is wave motion, so it seems that in all branches of industry alternating currents—electric wave motion—will have the sway.

One reason, perhaps, why this brand of science is being so rapidly developed is to be found in the interest which is attached to its experimental study. We wind a simple ring of iron with coils; we establish the connections to the generator, and with wonder and delight we note the effects of strange forces which we bring into play, which allow us to transform, to transmit and

---

* For Mr. Tesla's American Lecture on this subjects see THE ELECTRICAL WORLD of July 11, 1891, and for a report of his French lecture see THE ELECTRICAL WORLD of March 26, 1892.

direct energy at will. We arrange the circuits properly, and we see the mass of iron and wires behave as though it were endowed with life, spinning a heavy armature, through invisible connections, with great speed and power with the energy possibly conveyed from a great distance. We observe how the energy of an alternating current traversing the wire manifests itself—not so much in the wire as in the surrounding space—in the most surprising manner, taking the forms of heat, light, mechanical energy, and, most surprising of all, even chemical affinity. All these observations fascinate us, and fill us with an intense desire to know more about the nature of these phenomena. Each day we go to our work in the hope of discovering—in the hope that some one, no matter who, may find a solution of one of the pending great problems,—and each succeeding day we return to our task with renewed ardor; and even if we *are* unsuccessful, our work has not been in vain, for in these strivings, in these efforts, we have hours of untold pleasure, and we have directed our energies to the benefit of mankind.

We may take—at random, if you choose—any of the many experiments which may be performed with alternating currents; a few of which only, and by no means the mast striking, form the subject of this evening's demonstration; they are all equally interesting, equally inciting to thought.

Here is a simple glass tube from which the air has been partially exhausted. I take hold of it; I bring my body in contact with a wire conveying alternating currents of high potential, and the tube in my hand is brilliantly lighted. In whatever position I may put it, wherever I may move it in space, as far as I can reach, its soft, pleasing light persists with undiminished brightness.

Here is an exhausted bulb suspended from a single wire. Standing on an insulated support, I grasp it, and a platinum button mounted in it is brought to vivid incandescence.

Here, attached to a leading wire is another bulb, which, as I touch its metallic socket, is filled with magnificent colors of phosphorescent light.

Here still another, which by my fingers' touch casts a shadow—the Crookes shadow, of the stem inside of it.

Here, again, insulated as I stand on this platform, I bring my body in contact with one of the terminals of the secondary of this induction coil—with the end of a wire many miles long—and you see streams of light break forth from its distant end, which is set in violent vibration.

Here, once more, attach these two plates of wire gauze to the terminals of the coil, I set them a distance apart, and I set the coil to work. You may see a small spark pass between the plates. I insert a thick plate of one of the best dielectrics between them, and instead of rendering altogether impossible, as we are used to expect, I *aid* the passage of the discharge, which, as I insert the plate, merely changes in appearance and assumes the form of luminous streams.

Is there, I ask, can there be, a more interesting study than that of alternating currents?

In all these investigations, in all these experiments, which are so very, very interesting, for many years past—ever since the greatest experimenter who lectured in this hall discovered its principle—we have had a steady companion, an appliance familiar to every one, a plaything once, a thing of momentous importance now—the induction coil. There is no dearer appliance to the electrician. From the ablest among you, I dare say, down to the inexperienced student, to your lecturer, we all have passed many delightful hours in experimenting with the induction coil. We have watched its play, and thought and pondered over the beautiful phenomena which it disclosed to our ravished eyes. So well known is this apparatus, so familiar are these phenomena to every one, that my courage nearly fails me when I think that I have ventured to address so able an audience, that I have ventured to entertain you with that same old subject. Here in reality is the same apparatus, and here are the same phenomena, only the apparatus is operated somewhat differently, the phenomena are presented in a different aspect. Some of the results we find as expected, others surprise us, but all captivate our attention, for in scientific investigation each novel result achieved may be the centre of a new departure, each novel fact learned may lead to important developments.

Usually in operating an induction foil we have set up a vibration of moderate frequency in the primary, either by means of an interrupter or break, or by the use of an alternator. Earlier English investigators, to mention only Spottiswoode and J. E. H. Gordon, have used a rapid break in connection with the coil. Our knowledge and experience of to-day enables us to see clearly why these coils under the conditions of the tests did not disclose any remarkable phenomena, and why able experimenters failed to perceive many of the curious effects which have since been observed.

In the experiments such as performed this evening, we operate the coil either from a specially constructed alternator capable of giving many thousands of reversals of current per second, or, by disruptively discharging a condenser through the primary, we set up a vibration in the secondary circuit of a frequency of many hundred thousand or millions per second, if we so desire; and in using either of these means we enter a field as yet unexplored.

It is impossible to pursue an investigation in any novel line without finally making some interesting observation or learning some useful fact. That this statement is applicable to the subject of this lecture the many curious and unexpected phenomena which we observe afford a convincing proof. By way of illustration, take for instance the most obvious phenomena, those of the discharge of the induction coil.

Here is a coil which is operated by currents vibrating with extreme rapidity, obtained by disruptively discharging a Leyden jar. It would not surprise a student were the lecturer to say that the secondary of this coil consists of a small length of comparatively stout wire; it would not surprise him were the lecturer to state that, in spite of this, the coil is capable of giving any potential which the best insulation of the turns is able to withstand; but although he may be prepared, and even be indifferent as to the anticipated result, yet the aspect of the discharge of the coil will surprise and interest him. Every one is familiar with the discharge of an ordinary coil; it need not be reproduced here. But, by way of contrast, here is a form of discharge of a coil, the primary current of which is vibrating several hundred thousand times per second. The discharge of an ordinary coil appears as a simple line or band of light. The discharge of this coil appears in the form of powerful brushes and luminous streams issuing from all points of the two straight wires attached to the terminals of the secondary. (Fig. 1.)

Now compare this phenomenon which you have just witnessed with the discharge of a Holtz or Wimshurst machine—that other interesting appliance, so dear to the experimenter. What a difference there is between these phenomena! And yet, had I made the necessary arrangements—which could have been made easily, were it not that they would interfere with other experiments—I could have produced with this coil sparks which, had I the

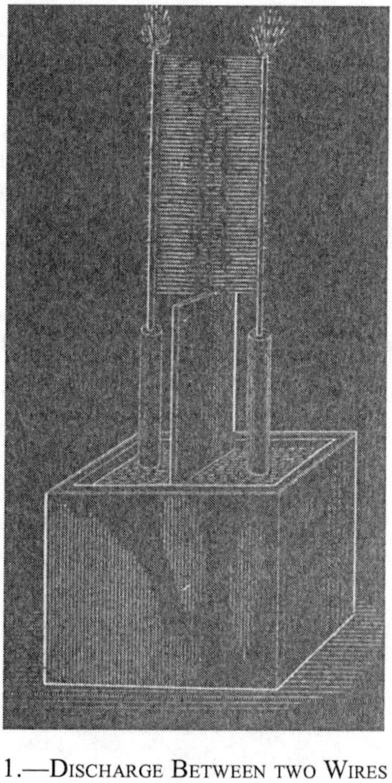

FIG. 1.—DISCHARGE BETWEEN TWO WIRES WITH FREQUENCIES OF A FEW HUNDRED THOUSAND PER SECOND.

coil hidden from your view and only two knobs exposed, even the keenest observer among you would find it difficult, if not impossible, to distinguish from those of an influence or friction machine. This may be done in many ways—for instance, by operating the induction coil which charges the condenser from an alternating-current machine of very low frequency, and preferably adjusting the discharge circuit so that there are no oscillations set up in it. We then obtain in the secondary circuit, if the knobs are of the required size and properly set, a more or less rapid succession of sparks of great intensity and small quantity, which possess the same brilliancy, and are accompanied by the same sharp crackling sound, as those obtained from a friction or influence machine.

Another way is to pass through two primary circuits, having a common secondary, two currents of a slightly different period, which produce in the secondary circuit sparks occurring at comparatively long intervals. But, even with the means at hand this evening, I may succeed in imitating the spark of a Holtz machine. For this purpose I establish between the terminals of the coil which charges the condenser a long, unsteady arc, which is periodically interrupted by the upward current of air produced by it. To increase the current of air I place on each side of the arc, and close to it, a large plate of mica. The condenser charged from this coil discharge into the primary circuit of a second coil through a small air gap, which is necessary to produce a sudden rush of current through the primary. The scheme of connections in the present experiment is indicated in Fig. 2.

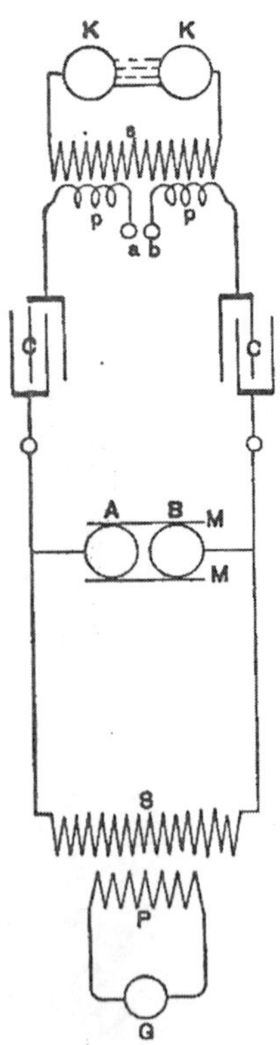

Fig. 2.—Imitating the Spark of a Holtz Machine.

G is an ordinarily constructed alternator, supplying the primary *P* of an induction coil, the secondary *S* of which charges the condensers or jars *C C*. The terminals of the secondary are connected to the inside coatings of the jars, the outer coatings being connected to the ends of the primary *p p* of a second induction coil. This primary *p p* has a small air gap *a b*.

The secondary *s* of this coil is provided with knobs or spheres *K K* of the proper size and set at a distance suitable for the experiment.

A long arc is established between the terminals *A B* of the first induction coil. *M M* are the mica plates.

Each time the arc is broken between *A* and *B* the jars are quickly charged and discharged through the primary *p p*, producing a snapping spark between the knobs *K K*. Upon the arc forming between *A* and *B* the potential falls, and the jars cannot be charged to such high potential as to break through the air gap *a b* until the arc is again broken by the draught.

In this manner sudden impulses, at long intervals, are produced in the primary *P P*, which in the secondary *s* give a corresponding number of impulses of great intensity. If the secondary knobs or spheres *K K* are of the proper size, the sparks show much resemblance to those of a Holtz machine. But these two effects, which to the eye appear so very different, are only two of the many discharge phenomena. We only need to change the conditions of the test, and again we make other observations of interest.

When, instead of operating the induction coil as in the last two experiments, we operate it from a high frequency alternator, as in the next experiment, a systematic study of the phenomena is rendered much more easy. In such case, in varying the strength and frequency of the currents through the primary, we may observe five distinct forms of discharge, which I have described in my former paper on the subject* before the American Institute of Electrical Engineers, May 20, 1891.

It would take too much time, and it would lead us too far from the subject presented this evening, to reproduce all these forms, but it seems to me desirable to show you one of them. It is a brush discharge, which is interesting in more than one respect. Viewed from a near position it resembles much a jet of gas escaping under great pressure. We know that the phenomenon is due to the agitation of the molecules near the terminal, and we anticipate that some heat must be developed by the impact of the molecules against the terminal or against each other. Indeed, we find that the brush is hot, and only a little thought leads us to the conclusion that, could we but reach sufficiently high frequencies, we could produce a brush which would give intense light and heat, and which would resemble in every particular an ordinary flame, save, perhaps, that both phenomena might not be due to the same agent—save, perhaps, that chemical affinity might not be *electrical* in its nature.

As the production of heat and light is here due to the impact of the molecules, or atoms of air, or something else besides, and, as we can augment the energy simply by raising the potential, we might, even with frequencies obtained from a dynamo machine, intensify the action to such a degree as to bring the terminal to melting heat. But with such low frequencies we would have to deal always with something of the nature of an electric current. If I approach a conducting object to the brush, a thin little spark passes, yet, even with the frequencies used this evening, the tendency to spark is not very great.

---

* *see* The Electrical World, July 11, 1891.

So, for instance, if I hold a metallic sphere at some distance above the terminal you may see the whole space between the terminal and sphere illuminated by the streams without the spark passing; and with the much higher frequencies obtainable by the disruptive discharge of a condenser, were it not for the sudden impulses, which are comparatively few in number, sparking would not occur even at very small distances. However, with incomparably higher frequencies, which we may yet find means to produce efficiently, and provided that electric impulses of such high frequencies could be transmitted through a conductor, the electrical characteristics of the brush discharge would completely vanish—no spark would pass, no shock would be felt—yet we would still have to deal with an *electric* phenomenon, but in the broad, modern interpretation of the word. In my first paper before referred to I have pointed out the curious properties of the brush, and described the best manner of producing it, but I have thought it worth while to endeavor to express myself more clearly in regard to this phenomenon, because of its absorbing interest.

When a coil is operated with currents of very high frequency, beautiful brush effects may be produced, even if the coil be of comparatively small dimensions. The experimenter may vary them in many ways, and, if it were nothing else, they afford a pleasing sight. What adds to their interest is that they may be produced with one single terminal as well as with two—in fact, often better with one than with two.

But of all the discharge phenomena observed, the most pleasing to the eye, and the most instructive, are those observed with a coil which is operated by means of the disruptive discharge of a condenser. The power of the brushes, the abundance of the sparks, when the conditions are patiently adjusted, is often amazing. With even a very small coil, if it be so well insulated as to stand a difference of potential of several thousand volts per turn, the sparks may be so abundant that the whole coil may appear a complete mass of fire.

Curiously enough the sparks, when the terminals of the coil are set at a considerable distance, seem to dart in every possible direction as though the terminals were perfectly independent of each other. As the sparks would soon destroy the insulation it is necessary to prevent them. This is best done by immersing the coil in a good liquid insulator, such as boiled-out oil. Immersion in a liquid may be considered almost an absolute necessity for the continued and successful working of such a coil.

It is, of course, out of the question, in an experimental lecture, with only a few minutes at disposal for the performance of each experiment, to show these discharge phenomena to advantage, as to produce each phenomenon at its best a very careful adjustment is required. But even if imperfectly produced, as they are likely to be this evening, they are sufficiently striking to interest an intelligent audience.

Before showing some of these curious effects I must, for the sake of completeness, give a short description of the coil and other apparatus used in the experiments with the disruptive discharge this evening.

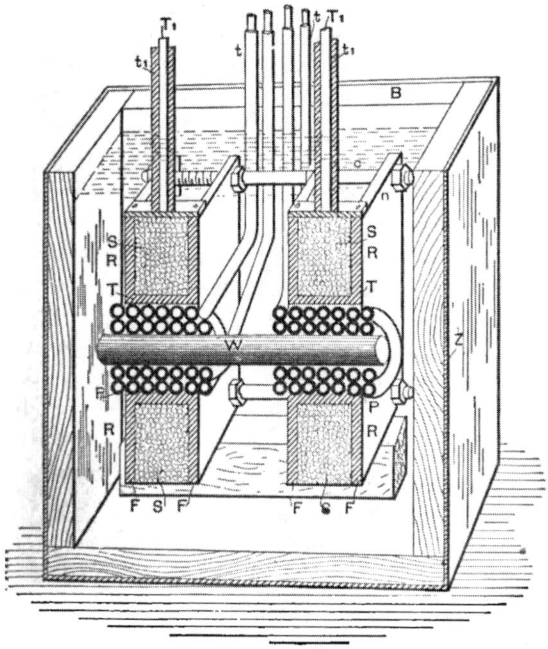

FIG. 3.—DISRUPTIVE DISCHARGE COIL.

It is contained in a box *B* (Fig. 3) of thick boards of hard wood, covered on the outside with zinc sheet *Z*, which is carefully soldered all around. It might be advisable, in a strictly scientific investigation, when accuracy is of great importance, to do away with the metal cover, as it might introduce many errors, principally on account of its complex action upon the coil, as a condenser of very small capacity and as an electrostatic and electromagnetic screen. When the coil is used for such experiments as are here contemplated, the employment of the metal cover offers some practical advantages, but these are not of sufficient importance to be dwelt upon.

The coil should be placed symmetrically to the metal cover, and the space between should, of course, not be too small, certainly not less than, say, five centimeters, but much more if possible; especially the two sides of the zinc box, which are at right angles to the axis of the coil, should be sufficiently remote from the latter, as otherwise they might impair its action and be a source of loss.

The coil consists of two spools of hard rubber *R R* held apart at a distance of 10 centimetres by bolts *c* and nuts *n*, likewise of hard rubber. Each spool comprises a tube *T* of approximately 8 centimetres inside diameter, and 3 millimetres thick, upon which are screwed two flanges F F, 24 centimetres square, the space between the flanges being about 3 centimetres. The secondary, *S S*, of the best gutta percha-covered wire, has 26 layers, 10 turns in each, giving for each half a total of 260 turns. The two halves are wound oppositely and connected in series, the connection between both being made over the primary. This disposition besides being convenient, has the advantage that when the coil is well balanced—that is, when both of its terminals T_1 T_1 are connected to bodies or devices of equal capacity—there is not much danger of breaking through to the primary, and the insulation between the primary and the secondary need not be thick. In using the coil it is advisable to attach to *both* terminals devices of nearly equal capacity, as, when the capacity of the terminals is not equal, sparks will be apt to pass to the primary. To avoid this, the middle point of the secondary may be connected to the primary, but this is not always practicable.

The primary *P P* is wound in two parts, and oppositely, upon a wooden spool *W*, and the four ends are led out of the oil through hard rubber tubes *t t*. The ends of the secondary T_1 T_1 are also led out of the oil through rubber tubes t_1 t_1 of great thickness. The primary and secondary layers are insulated by cotton cloth, the thickness of the insulation, of course, bearing some proportion to the difference of potential between the turns of the different layers. Each half of the primary has four layers, 24 turns in each, this giving a total of 96 turns. When both the parts are connected in series, this gives a ratio of conversion of about 1:2.7, and with the primaries in multiple, 1:5.4 but in operating with very rapidly alternating currents this ratio does not convey even an approximate idea of the ratio of the E.M.Fs. in the primary and secondary circuits. The coil is held in position in the oil on wooden supports, there being about 5 centimetres thickness of oil all round. Where the oil is not specially needed, the space is filled with pieces of wood, and for this purpose principally the wooden box B surrounding the whole is used.

The construction here shown is, of course, not the best on general principles, but I believe it is a good and convenient one for the production of effects in which an excessive potential and a very small current are needed.

In connection with the coil I use either the ordinary form of discharger or a modified form. In the former I have introduced two changes which secure some advantages, and which are obvious. If they are mentioned, it is only in the hope that some experimenter may find them of use.

One of the changes is that the adjustable knobs *A* and *B* (Fig. 4), of the discharger are held in jaws of brass, *J J*, by spring pressure, this allowing of

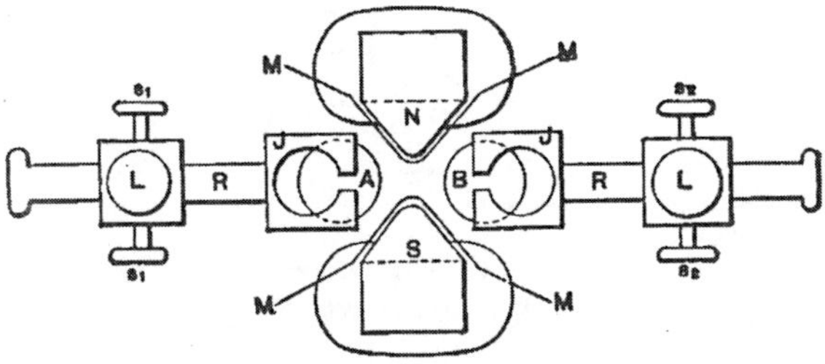

FIG. 4.—ARRANGEMENT OF IMPROVED DISCHARGER AND MAGNET.

turning them successively into different positions, and so doing away with the tedious process of frequent polishing up.

The other change consists in the employment of a strong electromagnet *N S*, which is placed with its axis at right angles to the line joining the knobs *A* and *B*, and produces a strong magnetic field between them. The pole pieces of the magnet are movable and properly formed so as to protrude between the brass knobs, in order to make the field as intense as possible; but to prevent the discharge from jumping to the magnet the pole pieces are protected by a layer of mica, *M M*, of sufficient thickness, $s_1 s_1$ and $s_2 s_2$ are screws for fastening the wires. On each side one of the screws is for large and the other for small wires. *L L* are screws for fixing in position the rods *R R*, which support the knobs.

In another arrangement with the magnet I take the discharge between the rounded pole pieces themselves, which in such case are insulated and preferably provided with polished brass caps.

The employment of an intense magnetic field is of advantage principally when the induction coil or transformer which charges the condenser is operated by currents of very low frequency. In such a case the number of the fundamental discharges between the knobs may be so small as to render the currents produced in the secondary unsuitable for many experiments. The intense magnetic field then serves to blow out the arc between the knobs as soon as it is formed, and the fundamental discharges occur in quicker succession.

Instead of the magnet, a draught or blast of air may be employed with some advantage. In this case the arc is preferably established between the knobs *A B*, in Fig. 2 (the knobs *a b* being generally joined, or entirely done away with), as in this disposition the arc is long and unsteady, and is easily affected by the draught.

When a magnet is employed to break the arc, it is better to choose the connection indicated diagrammatically in Fig 5, as in this case the currents forming the arc are much more powerful, and the magnetic field exercises a greater influence. The use of the magnet permits, however, of the arc being

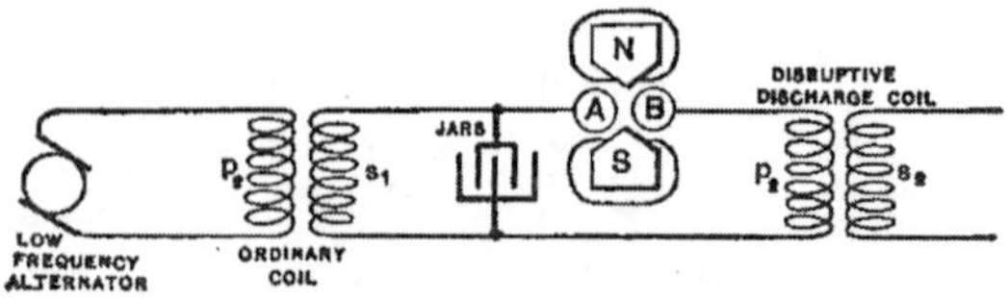

FIG. 5.—ARRANGEMENT WITH LOW-FREQUENCY ALTERNATOR AND IMPROVED DISCHARGER.

replaced by a vacuum tube, but I have encountered great difficulties in working with an exhausted tube.

The other form of discharger used in these and similar experiments is indicated in Figs. 6 and 7. It consists of a number of brass pieces *c c* (Fig. 6), each of which comprises a spherical middle portion m with an extension e

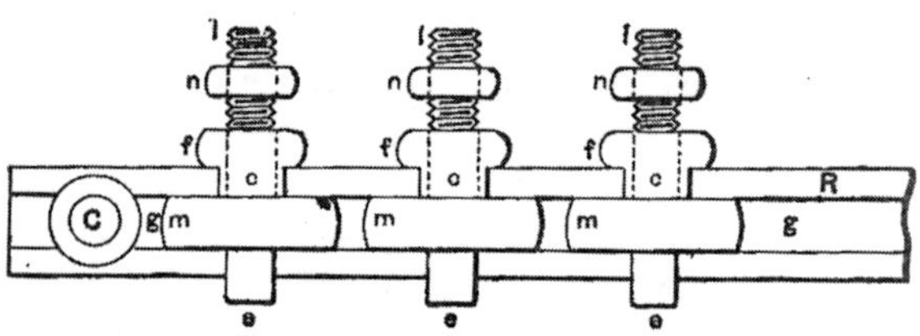

FIG. 6.—DISCHARGER WITH MULTIPLE GAPS.

below—which is merely used to fasten the piece in a lathe when polishing up the discharging surface—and a column above, which consists of a knurled flange f surmounted by a threaded stem I carrying a nut *n*, by means of which a wire is fastened to the column. The flange *f* conveniently serves for holding the brass piece when fastening the wire, and also for turning it in any position when it becomes necessary to present a fresh discharging surface. Two stout strips of hard rubber *R R*, with planed grooves *g g* (Fig. 7) to fit the middle

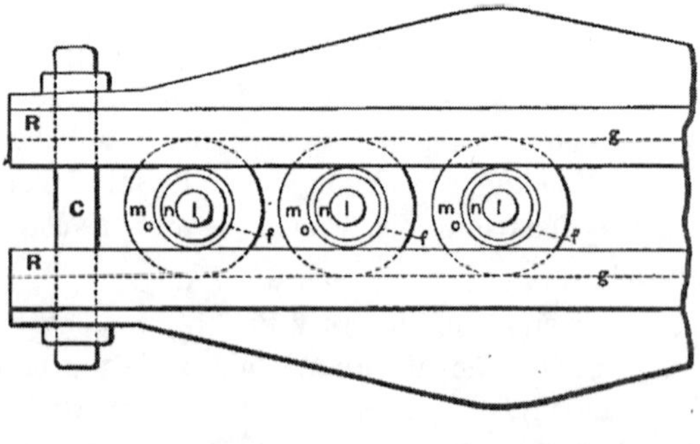

FIG. 7.—DISCHARGER WITH MULTIPLE GAPS.

portion of the pieces *c c*, serve to clamp the latter and hold them firmly in position by means of two bolts *C C* (of which only one is shown) passing through the ends of the strips.

In the use of this kind of discharger I have found three principal advantages over the ordinary form. First, the dielectric strength of a given total width of air space is greater when a great many small air gaps are used instead of one, which permits of working with a smaller length of air gap, and that means smaller loss and less deterioration of the metal; secondly by reason of splitting the arc up into smaller arcs, the polished surfaces are made to last much longer; and, thirdly, the apparatus affords some gauge in the experiments. I usually set the pieces by putting between them sheets of uniform thickness at a certain very small distance which is known from the experiments of Sir William Thomson to require a certain electromotive force to be bridged by the spark.

It should, of course, be remembered that the sparking distance is much diminished as the frequency is increased. By taking any number of spaces the experimenter has a rough idea of the electromotive force, and he finds it easier to repeat an experiment, as he has not the trouble of setting the knobs again and again. With this kind of discharger I have been able to maintain an oscillating motion without any spark being visible with the naked eye between the knobs, and they would not show a very appreciable rise in temperature. This form of discharger also lends itself to many arrangements of condensers and circuits which are often very convenient and timesaving. I have used it preferably in a disposition similar to that indicated in Fig. 2, when the currents forming the arcs are small.

I may here mention that I have also used dischargers with single or multiple air gaps, in which the discharge surfaces were rotated with great speed. No particular advantage was, however, gained by this method, except in cases where the currents from the condenser were large and the keeping cool of the surfaces was necessary, and in cases when, the discharge not being oscillating of itself, the arc as soon as established was broken by the air current, thus starting the vibration at intervals in rapid succession. I have also used mechanical interrupters in many ways. To avoid the difficulties with frictional contacts, the preferred plan adopted was to establish the arc and rotate through it at great speed a rim of mica provided with many holes and fastened to a steel plate. It is understood, of course, that the employment of a magnet, air current, or other interrupter, produces an effect worth noticing, unless the self-induction, capacity and resistance are so related that there are oscillations set up upon each interruption.

I will now endeavor to show you some of the most noteworthy of these discharge phenomena.

I have stretched across the room two ordinary cotton covered wires, each about 7 metres in length. They are supported on insulating cords at a distance of about 30 centimetres. I attach now to each of the terminals of the coil one of the wires and set the coil in action. Upon turning the lights off in the room you see the wires strongly illuminated by the streams issuing abundantly from their whole surface in spite of the cotton covering, which may even be very thick. When the experiment is performed under good conditions, the light from the wires is sufficiently intense to allow distinguishing the objects in a room. To produce the best result it is, of course, necessary to adjust carefully the capacity of the jars, the arc between the knobs and the length of the wires. My experience is that calculation of the length of the wires leads, in such case, to no result whatever. The experimenter will do best to take the wires at the start very long, and then adjust by cutting off first long pieces, and then smaller and smaller ones as he approaches the right length.

A convenient way is to use an oil condenser of very small capacity, consisting of two small adjustable metal plates, in connection with this and similar experiments. In such case I take wires rather short and set at the beginning the condenser plates at maximum distance. If the streams for the wires increase by approach of the plates, the length of the wires is about right; if they diminish the wires are too long for that frequency and potential. When a condenser is used in connection with experiments with such a coil, it should be an oil condenser by all means, as in using an air condenser considerable energy might be wasted. The wires leading to the plates in the oil should be very thin, heavily coated with some insulating compound, and provided with a conducting covering—this preferably extending under the surface of the oil. The conducting cover should not be too near the terminals, or ends, of the wire, as a spark would be apt to jump from the wire to it. The conducting coating is used to diminish the air losses, in virtue of its action as an electrostatic screen. As to the size of the vessel containing the oil and the site of the plates, the experimenter gains at once an idea from a rough trial. The size of the plates *in oil* is, however, calculable, as the dielectric losses are very small.

In the preceding experiment it is of considerable interest to know what relation the quantity of the light emitted bears to the frequency and potential of the electric impulses. My opinion is that the heat as well as light effects produced should be proportionate, under otherwise equal conditions of test, to the product of frequency and square of potential, but the experimental verification of the law, whatever it may be, would be exceedingly difficult. One thing is certain, at any rate, and that is, that in augmenting the potential and frequency we rapidly intensify the streams; and, though it may be very sanguine, it is surely not altogether hopeless to expect that we may succeed in producing a practical illuminant on these lines. We would then be simply using burners or flames, in which there would be no chemical process, no consumption of material, but merely a transfer of energy, and which would, in all probability emit more light and less heat than ordinary flames.

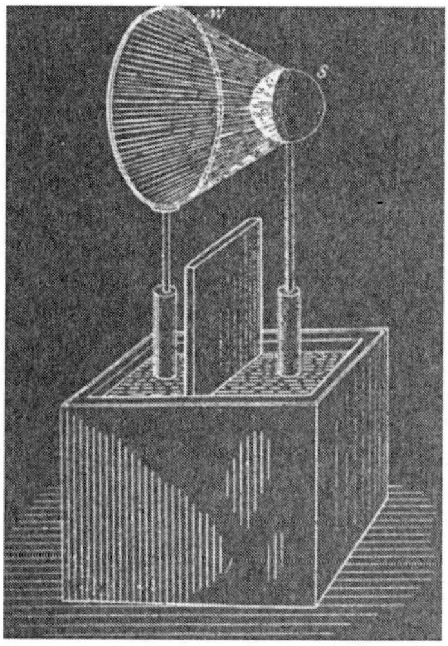

FIG. 8.—EFFECT PRODUCED BY CONCENTRATING STREAMS.

The luminous intensity of the streams is, of course, considerably increased when they are focused upon a small surface. This may be shown by the following experiment:

I attach to one of the terminals of the coil a wire w (Fig. 8), bent in a circle of about 30 centimetres in diameter, and to the other terminal I fasten a small brass sphere *s*, the surface of the wire being preferably equal to the surface of the sphere, and the centre of the latter being in a line at right angles to the plane of the wire circle and passing through its centre. When the discharge is established under proper conditions, a luminous hollow cone is formed, and in the dark one-half of the brass sphere is strongly illuminated, as shown in the cut.

By some artifice or other, it is easy to concentrate the streams upon small surfaces and to produce very strong light effects. Two thin wires may thus be rendered intensely luminous. In order to intensify the streams, the wires should be very thin and short; but as in this case their capacity would be generally too small for the coil—at least, for such a one as the present—it is necessary to augment the capacity to the required value, while, al the same time, the surface of the wires remains very small. This may be done in many ways.

Here, for instance, I have two plates *R R*, of hard rubber (Fig. 9), upon which I have glued two very thin wires *w w*, so as to form a name. The wires may be bare or covered with the best insulation—it is immaterial for the success of the experiment. Well-insulated wires, if anything, are preferable. On the back of each plate, indicated by the shaded portion, is a tinfoil coating *t t*.

Fig. 9.—Wires Rendered Intensely Luminous.

The plates are placed in line at a sufficient distance to prevent a spark passing from one to the other wire. The two tinfoil coatings I have joined by a conductor *C*, and the two wires I presently connect to the terminals of the coil. It is now easy, by varying the strength and frequency of the currents through the primary, to find a point at which the capacity of the system is best suited to the conditions, and the wires become so strongly luminous that, when the light in the room is turned off the name formed by them appears in brilliant letters.

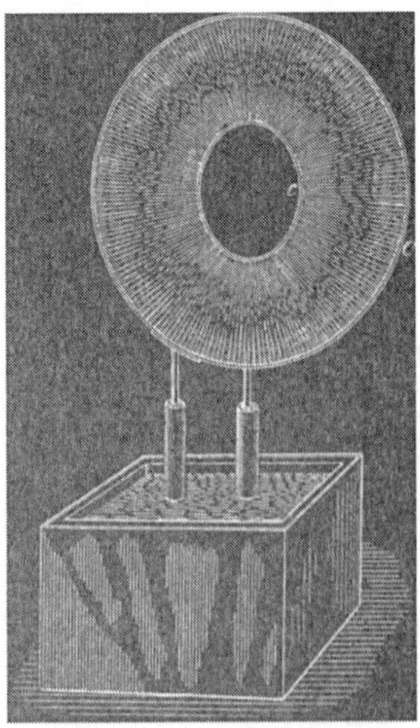

Fig. 10.—Luminous Discs.

It is perhaps preferable to perform this experiment with a coil operated from an alternator of high frequency, as then, owing to the harmonic rise and fall, the streams are very uniform, though they are less abundant than when produced with such a coil as the present. This experiment, however, may be performed with low frequencies, but much less satisfactorily.

When two wires, attached to the terminals of the coil, are set at the proper distance, the streams between them may be so intense as to produce a continuous luminous sheet. To show this phenomenon I have here two circles, C and *c* (Fig. 10), of rather stout wire, one being about 80 centimetres and the other 30 centimetres in diameter. To each of the terminals of the coil I attach one of the circles. The supporting wires are so bent that the circles may be placed in the same plane, coinciding as nearly as possible. When the light in the room is turned off and the coil set to work, you see the whole space between the wires uniformly filled with streams, forming a luminous disc, which could be seen from a considerable distance, such is the intensity of the streams. The outer circle could have been much larger than the present one; in fact, with this coil I have used much larger circles, and I have been able to produce a strongly luminous sheet, covering an area of more than one square metre, which is a remarkable effect with this very small coil. To avoid uncertainty, the circle has been taken smaller, and the area is now about 0.43 square metre.

The frequency of the vibration, and the quickness of succession of the sparks between the knobs, affect to a marked degree the appearance of the streams. When the frequency is very low, the air gives way in more or less the same manner, as by a steady difference of potential, and the streams consist of distinct threads, generally mingled with thin sparks, which probably correspond to the successive discharges occurring between the knobs. But when the frequency is extremely high, and the arc of the discharge produces a very *loud* but *smooth* sound—showing both that oscillation takes place and that the sparks succeed each other with great rapidity—then the luminous streams formed are perfectly uniform. To reach this result very small coils and jars of small capacity should be used. I take two tubes of thick Bohemian glass, about 5 centimetres in diameter and 20 centimetres long. In each of the tubes I slip a primary of very thick copper wire. On the top of each tube I wind a secondary of much thinner gutta-percha covered wire. The two secondaries I connect in series, the primaries preferably in multiple arc. The tubes are then placed in a large glass vessel, at a distance of l0 to 15 centimetres from each other, on insulating supports, and the vessel is filled with boiled out oil, the oil reaching about an inch above the tubes. The free ends of the secondary are lifted out of the oil and placed parallel to each other at a distance of about 10 centimetres. The ends which are scraped should be dipped in the oil. Two four-pint jars joined in series may be used to discharge through the primary. When the necessary adjustments in the length and distance of the wires above the oil and in the arc of discharge are made, a luminous sheet is produced between the wires, which is perfectly smooth and textureless, like the ordinary discharge through a moderately exhausted tube.

I have purposely dwelt upon this apparently insignificant experiment. In trials of this kind the experimenter arrives at the startling conclusion that, to pass ordinary luminous discharges through gases, no particular degree of exhaustion is needed, but that the gas may be at ordinary or even greater pressure. To accomplish this, a very high frequency is essential; a high potential is likewise required, but this is a merely incidental necessity. These experiments teach us that, in endeavoring to discover novel methods of producing light by the agitation of atoms, or molecules, of a gas, we need not limit our research to the vacuum tube, but may look forward quite seriously to the possibility of obtaining the light effects without the use of any vessel whatever, with air at ordinary pressure.

Such discharges of very high frequency, which render luminous the air at ordinary pressures, we have probably often occasion to witness in Nature. I have no doubt that if, as many believe, the aurora borealis is produced by sudden cosmic disturbances, such as eruptions at the sun's surface, which set the electrostatic charge of the earth in an extremely rapid vibration the red glow observed is not confined to the upper rarefied strata of the air, but the discharge traverses, by reason of its very high frequency, also the dense atmosphere in the form of a *glow*, such as we ordinarily produce in a slightly exhausted tube. If the frequency were very low or even more so, if the charge were not at all vibrating, the dense air would break down as in a lightning discharge. Indications of such breaking down of the lower dense strata of the air have been repeatedly observed at the occurrence of this marvelous phenomenon; but if it does occur; it can only be attributed to the fundamental disturbances, which are few in number, for the vibration produced by them would be far too rapid to allow a disruptive break. It is the original and irregular impulses which affect the instruments; the superimposed vibrations probably pass unnoticed.

When an ordinary low frequency discharge is passed through moderately rarefied air, the air assumes a purplish hue. If by some means or other we increase the intensity of the molecular, or atomic, vibration, the gas changes to a white color. A similar change occurs at ordinary pressures with electric impulses of very high frequency. If the molecules of the air around a wire are moderately agitated, the brush formed is reddish or violet; if the vibration is rendered sufficiently intense, the streams become white. We may accomplish this in various ways. In the experiment before shown with the two wires across the room, I have endeavored to secure the result by pushing to a high value both the frequency and potential; in the experiment with the thin wires glued on the rubber plate I have concentrated the action upon a very small surface—in other words, I have worked with a great electric density.

A most curious form of discharge is observed with such a coil when the frequency and potential are pushed to the extreme limit. To perform the experiment, every part of the coil should be heavily insulated, and only two small spheres—or, better still, two sharp-edged metal discs (*d d*, Fig. 11) of no more than a few centimetres in diameter—should be exposed to the air. The coil here used immersed in oil, and the ends of the secondary reaching out of the oil are covered with an airtight cover of hard rubber of great thickness. All cracks, if there are any, should be carefully stopped up, so that the brush discharge cannot form anywhere except on the small spheres or plates which are exposed to the air. In this case, since there are no large plates or other bodies of capacity attached to the terminals, the coil is capable of an extremely rapid vibration. The potential may be raised by increasing, as far as the experimenter judges proper, the rate of change of the primary current. With a coil not widely differing from the present, it is best to connect the two primaries in multiple arc; but if the secondary should have a much greater number of turns the primaries should preferably be used in series, as otherwise the vibration might be too fast for the secondary. It occurs under these conditions that misty white streams break forth from the edges of the discs and spread out phantom-like into space. With this coil, when fairly well produced, they are about 25 to 30 centimetres long. When the hand is held

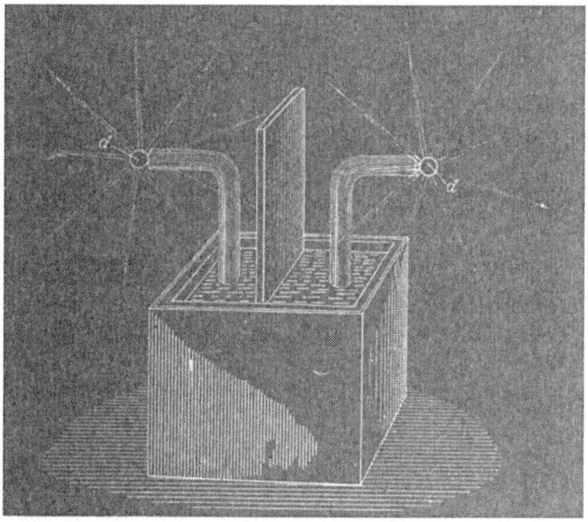

Fig. 11.—Phantom Streams.

against them no sensation is produced, and a spark, causing a shock, jumps from the terminal only upon the hand being brought much nearer. If the oscillation of the primary current is rendered intermittent by some means or other, there is a corresponding throbbing of the streams, and now the hand or other conducting object may be brought in still greater proximity to the terminal without a spark being caused to jump.

Among the many beautiful phenomena which may be produced with such a coil I have here selected only those which appear to possess some features of novelty, and lead us to some conclusions of interest. One will not find it at all difficult to produce in the laboratory, by means of it, many other phenomena which appeal to the eye even more than these here shown, but present no particular feature of novelty.

Early experimenters describe the display of sparks produced by an ordinary large induction coil upon an insulating plate separating the terminals. Quite recently Siemens performed some experiments in which fine effects were obtained, which were seen by many with interest. No doubt large coils, even if operated with currents of low frequencies, are capable of producing beautiful effects. But the largest coil ever made could not, by far, equal the magnificent display of streams and sparks obtained from such a disruptive discharge coil when properly adjusted. To give an idea, a coil such as the present one will cover easily a plate of 1 metre in diameter completely with the streams. The best way to perform such experiments is to take a very thin rubber or a glass plate and glue on one side of it a narrow ring of tinfoil of very large diameter, and on the other a circular washer, the centre of the latter coinciding with that of the ring, and the surfaces of both being preferably equal, so as to keep the coil well balanced. The washer and ring should be connected to the terminals by heavily insulated thin wires. It is easy in observing the effect of the capacity to produce a sheet of uniform streams, or a fine network of thin silvery threads, or a mass of loud brilliant sparks, which completely cover the plate.

Since I have advanced the idea of the conversion by means of the disruptive discharge, in my paper before the American Institute of Electrical Engineers at the beginning of the past year, the interest excited in it has been considerable. It affords us a means for producing any potentials by the aid of inexpensive coils operated from ordinary systems of distribution, and—what is perhaps more appreciated—it enables us to convert currents of any frequency into currents of any other lower or higher frequency. But its chief value will perhaps be found in the help which it will afford us in the investigations of the phenomena of phosphorescence, which a disruptive discharge coil is capable of exciting in innumerable cases where ordinary coils, even the largest, would utterly fail.

Considering its probable uses for many practical purposes, and its possible introduction into laboratories for scientific research, a few additional remarks as to the construction of such a coil will perhaps not be found superfluous.

It is, of course, absolutely necessary to employ in such a coil wires provided with the best insulation.

Good coils may be produced by employing wires covered with several layers of cotton, boiling the coil a long time in pure wax, and cooling under moderate pressure. The advantage of such a coil is that it can be easily handled, but it cannot probably give as satisfactory results as a coil immersed in pure oil. Besides, it seems that the presence of a large body of wax affects the coil disadvantageously, whereas this does not seem to be the case with oil. Perhaps it is because the dielectric losses in the liquid are smaller.

I have tried at first silk and cotton covered wires with oil immersion; but I have been gradually led to use gutta-percha covered wires, which proved most satisfactory. Gutta-percha insulation adds, of course, to the capacity of the coil, and this, especially if the coil be large, is a great disadvantage when extreme frequencies are desired; but, on the other hand, gutta-percha will withstand much more than an equal thickness of oil, and this advantage should be secured at any price. Once the coil has been immersed, it should never be taken out of the oil for more than a few hours, else the gutta-percha will crack up and the coil will not be worth half as much as before. Gutta-percha is probably slowly attacked by the oil, but after an immersion of eight to nine months I have found no ill effects.

I have obtained in commerce two kinds of gutta-percha wire: in one the insulation sticks tightly to the metal, in the other it does not. Unless a special method is followed to expel all air, it is much safer to use the first kind. I wind the coil within an oil tank so that all interstices are filled up with the oil. Between the layers I use cloth boiled out thoroughly in oil, calculating the thickness according to the difference of potential between the turns. There seems not to be a very great difference whatever kind of oil is used; I use paraffin or linseed oil.

To exclude more perfectly the air, an excellent way to proceed, and easily practicable with small coils, is the following: Construct a box of hard wood of very thick boards which have been for a long time boiled in oil. The boards should be so joined as to safely withstand the external air pressure. The coil being placed and fastened in position within the box, the latter is closed with a strong lid, and covered with closely fitting metal sheets, the joints of which are soldered very carefully. On the top two small holes are drilled, passing through the metal sheet and the wood, and in these holes two small glass tubes are inserted and the joints made air-tight. One of the tubes is connected to a vacuum pump and the other with a vessel containing a sufficient quantity of boiled-out oil. The latter tube has a very small hole at the bottom, and is provided with a stopcock. When a fairly good vacuum has been obtained, the stopcock is opened and the oil slowly fed in. Proceeding in this manner, it is impossible that any big bubbles, which are the principal danger, should remain between the turns. The air is most completely excluded, probably better than by boiling out, which, however, when gutta-percha coated wires are used, is not practicable.

For the primaries I use ordinary line wire with thick cotton coating. Strands of very thin insulated wires properly interlaced would, of course, be the best to employ for the primaries, but they are not to be had.

In an experimental coil the size of the wires is not of great importance. In the coil here used the primary is No, 12 and the secondary No. 24 Brown & Sharpe gauge wire; but the sections maybe varied considerably. I would only imply different adjustments; the results aimed at would not be materially affected.

I have dwelt at some length upon the various forms of brush discharge because, in studying them, we not only observe phenomena which please our eye, but also afford us food for thought, and lead us to conclusions of practical importance. In the use of alternating currents of very high tension, too much precaution cannot be taken to prevent the brush discharge. In a main conveying such currents, in an induction coil or transformer, or in a condenser, the brush discharge is a source of great danger to the insulation. In a condenser especially the gaseous matter must be most carefully expelled, for in it the charged surfaces are near each other, and if the potentials are high, just as sure as a weight will fall if let go, so the insulation will give way if a single gaseous bubble of some site be present, whereas, if all gaseous matter were carefully excluded, the condenser would safely withstand a much higher difference of potential. A main conveying alternating currents of very high tension may be injured merely by a blowhole or small crack in the insulation, the more so as a blowhole is apt to contain gas at low pressure; and as it appears almost impossible to completely obviate such little imperfections, I am led to believe that in our future distribution of electrical energy by currents of very high tension liquid insulation will be used. The cost is a great drawback, but if we employ an oil as an insulator the distribution of electrical energy with something like 100,000 volts, and even more, become, at least with higher frequencies, so easy that they could be hardly called engineering feats. With oil insulation and alternate current motors transmissions of power can be effected with safety and upon an industrial basis at distances of as much as a thousand miles.

A peculiar property of oils, and liquid insulation in general, when subjected to rapidly changing electric stresses, is to disperse any gaseous bubbles which may be present, and diffuse them through its mass, generally long before any injurious break can occur. This feature may be easily observed with an ordinary induction coil by taking the primary out, plugging up the end of the tube upon which the secondary is wound, and fining it with some fairly transparent insulator, such as paraffin oil. A primary of s diameter something like six millimetres smaller than the inside of the tube may be inserted in the oil. When the coil is set to work one may see, looking from the top through the oil, many luminous points—air bubbles which are caught by inserting the primary, and which ate rendered luminous in consequence of the violent bombardment. The occluded air, by its impact against the oil, beats it; the oil begins to circulate, carrying some of the air along with it, until the bubbles are dispersed and the luminous points disappear. In this manner, unless large bubbles are occluded in such way that circulation is rendered impossible, a damaging break is averted, the only effect being a moderate warming up of the oil. If, instead of the liquid, a solid insulation, no matter how thick, were used, a breaking through and injury of the apparatus would be inevitable.

The exclusion of gaseous matter from any apparatus in which the dielectric is subjected to more or less rapidly changing electric forces is, however, not only desirable in order to avoid a possible injury of the apparatus, but also on account of economy. In a condenser, for instance, as long as only a solid or only a liquid dielectric is used, the loss is small; but if a gas under ordinary or small pressure be present the loss may be very great. Whatever the nature of the force acting in the dielectric may be, it seems that in a solid or liquid the molecular displacement produced by the force is small: hence the product of force and displacement is insignificant, unless the force be very great; but in a gas the displacement, and, therefore, this product is considerable; the molecules are free to move, they reach high speeds, and the energy of their impact is lost in heat or otherwise. If the gas be strongly compressed, the displacement due to thc force is made smaller, and the losses are reduced.

In most of the succeeding experiments I prefer, chiefly on account of the regular and positive action, to employ the alternator before referred to. This is one of the several machines constructed by me for the purposes of these investigations. It has 384 pole projections, and is capable of giving currents of a frequency of about 10,000 per second. This machine has been illustrated and briefly described in my first paper before the American Institute of Electrical Engineers, May 20, 1831, to which I have already referred. A more detailed description, sufficient to enable any engineer to build a similar machine, will be found in several electrical journals of that period.

The induction coils operated from the machine are rather small, containing from 5,000 to 15,000 turns in the secondary. They are immersed in boiled-out linseed oil, contained in wooden boxes covered with zinc sheet.

I have found it advantageous to reverse the usual position of the wires, and to wind, in these coils, the primaries on the top; this allowing the use of a much bigger primary, which, of course, reduces the danger of overheating and increases the output of the coil. I make the primary on each side at least one centimetre shorter than the secondary, to prevent the breaking through on the ends, which would surely occur unless the insulation on the top of the secondary be very thick, and this, of course, would be disadvantageous.

When the primary is made movable, which is necessary in some experiments, and many times convenient for the purposes of adjustment, I cover the secondary with wax, and turn it off in a lathe to a diameter slightly smaller than the inside of the primary coil. The latter I provide with a handle reaching out of the oil, which serves to shift it in any position along the secondary.

I will now venture to make, in regard to the general manipulation of induction coils, a few observations bearing upon points which have not been fully appreciated in earlier experiments with such coils, and are even now often overlooked.

The secondary of the coil possesses usually such a high self-induction that the current through the wire is inappreciable, and may be so even when the terminals ate joined by a conductor of small resistance. If capacity is added to the terminals, the self-induction is counteracted, and a stronger current is made to flow through the secondary, though its terminals are insulated from each other. To one entirely unacquainted with the properties of alternating currents nothing will look more puzzling. This feature was illustrated in the experiment performed at the beginning with the top plates of wire gauze attached to the terminals and the rubber plate. When the plates of wire gauze were close together, and a small arc passed between them, the arc *prevented* a strong current from passing through the secondary, because it did away with the capacity on the terminals; when the rubber plate was inserted between, the capacity of the condenser formed counteracted the self-induction of the secondary, a stronger current passed now, the coil performed more work, and the discharge was by far more powerful.

The first thing, then, in operating the induction coil is to combine capacity with the secondary to overcome the self-induction. If the frequencies and potentials are very high gaseous matter should be carefully kept away from the charged surfaces. If Leyden jars are used, they should be immersed in oil, as otherwise considerable dissipation may occur if the jars are greatly strained. When high frequencies are used, it is of equal importance to combine a condenser with the primary. One may use a condenser connected to the ends of the primary or to the terminals of the alternator, but the latter is not to be recommended, as the machine might be injured. The best way is undoubtedly to use the condenser in series with the primary and with the alternator, and to adjust its capacity so as to annul the self-induction of both the latter. The condenser should be adjustable by very small steps, and for a finer adjustment a small oil condenser with movable plates may be used conveniently.

I think it best at this juncture to bring before you a phenomenon, observed by me some time ago, which to the purely scientific investigator may perhaps appear more interesting than any of the results which I have the privilege to present to you this evening.

It may be quite properly ranked among the brush phenomena—in fact, it is a brush, formed at, or near, a single terminal in high vacuum.

In bulbs provided with a conducting terminal, though it be of aluminium, the brush has but an ephemeral existence, and cannot, unfortunately, be indefinitely preserved in its most sensitive state, even in a bulb devoid of any conducting electrode. In studying one phenomenon, by all means a bulb having no leading-in wire should be used. I have found it best to use bulbs constructed as indicated in Figs. 12 and 13.

In Fig. 12 the bulb comprises an incandescent lamp globe *L*, in the neck of which is sealed a barometer tube *b*, the end of which is blown out to form a small sphere *s*. This sphere should be sealed as closely as possible in the centre of the large globe. Before sealing, a thin tube *t*, of aluminium sheet, may be slipped in the barometer tube, but it is not important to employ it.

The small hollow sphere *s* is filled with some conducting powder, and a wire *w* is cemented in the neck for the purpose of connecting the conducting powder with the generator.

The construction shown in Fig. 13 was chosen in order to remove from the brush any conducting body which might possibly affect it. The bulb consists in this case of a lamp globe *L*, which has a neck *n*, provided with a tube *b* and small sphere *s*, sealed to it, so that two entirely independent compartments are formed, as indicated in the drawing. When the bulb is in use, the neck *n* is provided with a tinfoil coating, which is connected to the generator and acts

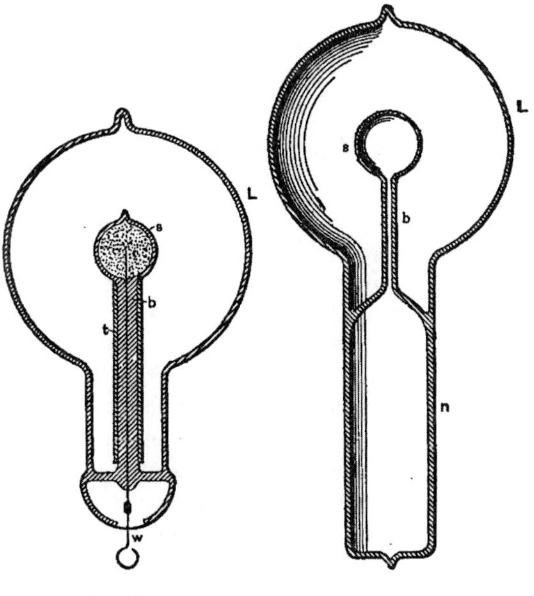

FIG. 12. FIG. 13.

BULBS FOR PRODUCING ROTATING BRUSH.

inductively upon the moderately rarefied and highly conducting gas enclosed in the neck. From there the current passes through the tube *b* into the small sphere *s*, to act by induction upon the gas contained in the globe *L*.

It is of advantage to make the tube *t* very thick, the hole through it very small, and to blow the sphere *s* very thin. It is of the greatest importance that the sphere *s* be placed in the centre of the globe *L*.

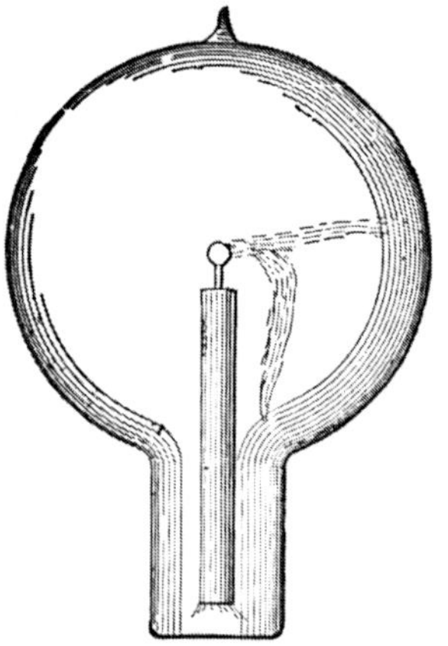

FIG. 14.—FORMS AND PHASES OF THE ROTATING BRUSH.

Figs. 14, 15 and 16 indicate different forms, or stages, of the brush. Fig. 14 shows the brush as it first appears in a bulb provided with a conducting terminal: but, as in such a bulb it very soon disappears—often after a few minutes—I will confine myself to the description of the phenomenon as seen in a bulb without conducting electrode. It is observed under the following conditions:

When the globe *L* (Figs. 12 and 13) is exhausted to a very high degree, generally the bulb is not excited upon connecting the wire *w* (Fig. 12) or the tinfoil coating of the bulb (Fig. 13) to the terminal of the induction coil. To excite it, it is usually sufficient to grasp the globe *L* with the hand. An intense phosphorescence then spreads at first over the globe, but soon gives place to a white, misty light. Shortly afterward one may notice that the luminosity is unevenly distributed in the globe, and after passing the current for some time the bulb appears as in Fig. 15. From this stage the phenomenon will gradually pass to that indicated in Fig. 16, after some minutes, hours, days or weeks, according as the bulb is worked. Warming the bulb or increasing the potential hastens the transit.

When the brush assumes the form indicated in Fig. 16, it may be brought to a state of extreme sensitiveness to electrostatic and magnetic influence.

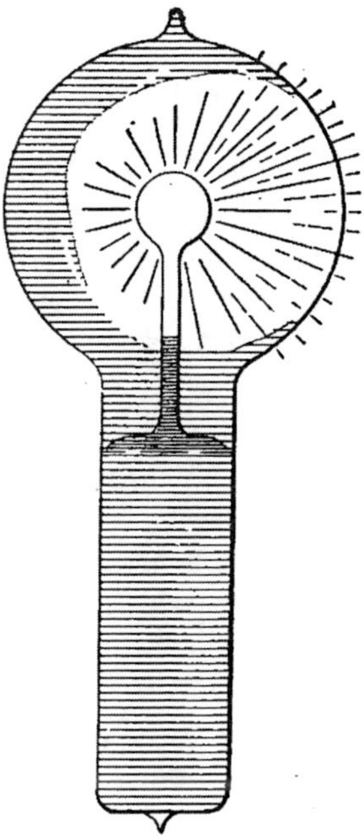

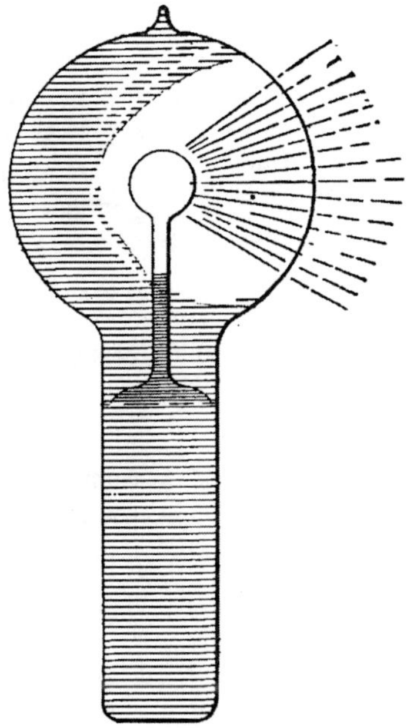

FIG. 15. FIG. 16.

FORMS AND PHASES OF THE ROTATING

The bulb hanging straight down from a wire, and all objects being remote from it, the approach of the observer at a few paces from the bulb will cause the brush to fly to the opposite side, and if he walks around the bulb it will always keep on the opposite side. It may begin to spin around the terminal long before it reaches that sensitive stage. When it begins to turn around principally, but also before, it is affected by a magnet and at a certain stage it is susceptible to magnetic influence to an astonishing degree. A small permanent magnet, with its poles at a distance of no more than two centimetres, will affect it visibly at a distance of two metres, slowing down or accelerating the rotation according to how it is held relatively to the brush. I think I have observed that at the stage when it is most sensitive to magnetic, it is not most sensitive to electrostatic, influence. My explanation is, that the electrostatic attraction between the brush and the glass of the bulb, which retards the rotation, grows much quicker than the magnetic influence when the intensity of the stream is increased.

When the bulb hangs with the globe *L* down, the rotation is always clockwise. In the southern hemisphere it would occur in the opposite direction and on the equator the brush should not turn at all. The rotation may be reversed by a magnet kept at some distance. The brush rotates best, seemingly, when it is at right angles to the lines of force of the earth. It very likely rotates, when at its maximum speed, in synchronism with the alternations, say 10,000 times a second. The rotation can be slowed down or accelerated by the approach or receding of the observer or any conducting body, but it cannot be reversed by putting the bulb in any position. When it is in the state of the highest sensitiveness and the potential or frequency be varied the sensitiveness is rapidly diminished. Changing either of these but little will generally stop the rotation. The sensitiveness is likewise affected by the variations of temperature. To attain great sensitiveness it is necessary to have the small sphere s in the centre of the globe *L*, as otherwise the electrostatic action of the glass of the globe will tend to stop the rotation. The sphere *s* should be small and of uniform thickness; any dissymmetry of course has the effect to diminish the sensitiveness.

The fact that the brush rotates in a definite direction in a permanent magnetic field seems to show that in alternating currents of very high frequency the positive and negative impulses are not equal, but that one always preponderates over the other.

Of course, this rotation in one direction may be due to the action of two elements of the same current upon each other, or to the action of the field produced by one of the elements upon the other, as in a series motor, without necessarily one impulse being stronger than the other. The fact that the brush turns, as far as I could observe, in any position, would speak for this view. In such case it would turn at any point of the earth's surface. But, on the other hand, it is then hard to explain why a permanent magnet should reverse the rotation, and one must assume the preponderance of impulses of one kind.

As to the causes of the formation of the brush or stream, I think it is due to the electrostatic action of the globe and the dissymmetry of the parts. If the small bulb s and the globe *L* were perfect concentric spheres, and the glass throughout of the same thickness and quality, I think the brush would not form, as the tendency to pass would be equal on all sides. That the formation of the stream is due to an irregularity is apparent from the fact that it has the tendency to remain in one position, and rotation occurs most generally only when it is brought out of this position by electrostatic or magnetic influence. When in an extremely sensitive state it rests in one position, most curious experiments may be performed with it. For instance, the experimenter may, try selecting a proper position, approach the hand at a certain considerable distance to the bulb, and he may cause the brush to pass off by merely stiffening the muscles of the arm. When it begins to rotate slowly, and the hands are held at a proper distance, it is impossible to make even the slightest motion without producing a visible effect upon the brush. A metal plate connected to the other terminal of the coil affects it at a great distance, slowing down the rotation often to one turn a second.

I am firmly convinced that such a brush, when we learn how to produce it properly, will prove a valuable aid in the investigation' of the nature of the forces acting in an electrostatic or magnetic field. If there is any motion which is measurable going on in the space, such a brush ought to reveal it. It is, so to speak, a beam of light, frictionless, devoid of inertia.

I think that it may find practical applications in telegraphy. With such a brush it would be possible to send dispatches across the Atlantic, for instance, with any speed, since its sensitiveness may be so great that the slightest changes will affect it. If it were possible to make the stream more intense and very narrow, its deflections could be easily photographed.

I have been interested to find whether there is a rotation of the stream itself, or whether there is simply a stress traveling around in the bulb. For this purpose I mounted a light mica fan so that its vanes were in the path of the brush. If the stream itself was rotating the fan would be spun around. I could produce no distinct rotation of the fan, although I tried the experiment repeatedly; but as the fan exerted a noticeable influence on the stream, and the apparent rotation of the latter was, in this case, never quite satisfactory, the experiment did not appear to be conclusive.

I have been unable to produce the phenomenon with the disruptive discharge coil, although every other of these phenomena can be tell produced by it—many, in fact, much better than with coils operated from an alternator.

It may be possible to produce the brush by impulses of one direction, or even by a steady potential, in which case it would be still more sensitive to magnetic influence.

In operating an induction coil with rapidly alternating currents, we realize with astonishment, for the first time, the great importance of the relation of capacity, self-induction and frequency as regards the general result. The effects of capacity are the most striking, for in these experiments, since the self-induction and frequency both are high, the critical capacity is very small, and need be but slightly varied to produce a very considerable change. The experimenter may bring his body in contact with the terminals of the secondary of the coil, or attach to one or both terminals insulated bodies of very small bulk, such as bulbs, and he may produce a considerable rise or fall of potential, and greatly affect the flow of the current through the primary. In the experiment before shown, in which a brush appears at a wire attached to one terminal, and the wire is vibrated when the experimenter brings his insulated body in contact with the other terminal of the coil, the sudden rise of potential was made evident.

I may show you the behavior of the coil in another manner which possesses a feature of some interest. I have here a little light fan of aluminium sheet, fastened to a needle and arranged to rotate freely in a metal piece screwed to one of the terminals of the coil. When the coil is set to work, the molecules of the air are rhythmically attracted and repelled. As the force with which they are repelled is greater than that with which they are attracted, it results that there is repulsion exerted on the surfaces of the fan. If the fan were made simply of a metal sheet, the repulsion would be equal on the opposite sides, and would produce no effect. But if one of the opposite surfaces is screened, or if, generally speaking, the bombardment on this side is weakened in some wag or other, there remains the repulsion exerted upon the other, and the fan is set in rotation. The screening is best effected by fastening upon one of the opposing sides of the fan insulated conducting coatings, or, if the fan is made in the shape of an ordinary propeller screw, by fastening on one side, and close to it, an insulated metal plate. The static screen may however, be omitted and simply a thickness of insulating material fastened to one of the sides of the fan.

To show the behavior of the coil, the fan may be placed upon the terminal and it will readily rotate when the coil is operated by currents of very high frequency. With a steady potential, of course, and even with alternating currents of very low frequency, it would not turn, because of the very slow exchange of air and, consequently, smaller bombardment; but in the latter case it might turn if the potential were excessive. With a pin wheel, quite the opposite rule holds good; it rotates best with a steady potential, and the effort is the smaller the higher the frequency. Now, it is very easy to adjust the conditions so that the potential is normally not sufficient to turn the fan, but that by connecting the other terminal of the coil with an insulated body it rises to a much greater value, so as to rotate the fan, and it is likewise possible to stop the rotation by connecting to the terminal a body of different size, thereby diminishing the potential.

Instead of using the fan in this experiment, we may use the "electric" radiometer with similar effect. But in this case it will be found that the vanes will rotate only at high exhaustion or at ordinary pressures; they will not rotate at moderate pressures, when the air is highly conducting. This curious observation was made conjointly by Professor Crookes and myself. I attribute the result to the high conductivity of the air, the molecules of which then do not act as independent carriers of electric charges, but act all together as a single conducting body. In such case, of course, if there is any repulsion at all of the molecules from the vanes, it must be very small. It is possible, however, that the result is in part due to the fact that the greater part of the discharge passes from the leading-in wire through the highly conducting gas, instead of passing off from the conducting vanes.

In trying the preceding experiment with the electric radiometer the potential should not exceed a certain limit, as then the electrostatic attraction between the vanes and the glass of the bulb may be so great as to stop the rotation.

A most curious feature of alternate currents of high frequencies and potentials is that they enable us to perform many experiments by the use of one wire only. In many respects this feature is of great interest.

In a type of alternate current motor invented by me some years ago I produced rotation by inducing, by means of a single alternating current passed through a motor circuit, in the mass or other circuits of the motor, secondary currents, which, jointly with the primary or inducing current, created n moving field of force. A simple but crude form of such a motor is obtained by winding upon an iron core a primary, and close to it a secondary coil, joining the ends of the latter and placing a freely movable metal disc within the influence of the field produced by both. The iron core is employed for obvious reasons, but it is not essential to the operation. To improve the motor, the iron core is made to encircle the armature. Again to improve, the secondary coil is made to overlap partly the primary, so that it cannot free itself from a strong inductive action of the latter, repel its lines as it may. Once more to improve, the proper difference of phase is obtained between the primary and secondary currents by a condenser, self-induction, resistance or equivalent windings.

I had discovered, however, that rotation is produced by means of a single coil and core; my explanation of the phenomenon, and leading thought in trying the experiment, being that there must be a true time lag in the magnetization of the core. I remember the pleasure I had when, in the writings of Professor Ayrton, which came later to my hand, I found the idea of the time lag advocated. Whether there is a true time lag, whether the retardation is due to eddy currents circulating in minute paths, must remain an open question, but the fact is that a coil wound upon an iron core and traversed by an alternating current creates a moving field of force, capable of setting an armature in rotation. It is of some interest, in conjunction with the historical Arago experiment, to mention that in lag or phase motors I have produced rotation in the opposite direction to the moving field, which means that in that experiment the magnet may not rotate, or may even rotate in the opposite direction to the moving disc. Here, then, is a motor (diagrammatically illustrated in Fig. 17/146), comprising a coil and iron core, and a freely movable copper disc in proximity to the latter.

To demonstrate a novel and interesting feature, I have, for a reason which I will explain, selected this type of motor. When the ends of the coil are connected to the terminals of an alternator the disc is set in rotation. But it is not this experiment, now well known, which I desire to perform. What I wish to show you is that this motor rotates with *one single* connection between it and the generator; that is to say, one terminal of the motor is connected to one terminal of the generator—in this case the secondary of a high-tension induction coil—the other terminals of motor and generator being insulated in space. To produce rotation it is generally (but not absolutely) necessary to

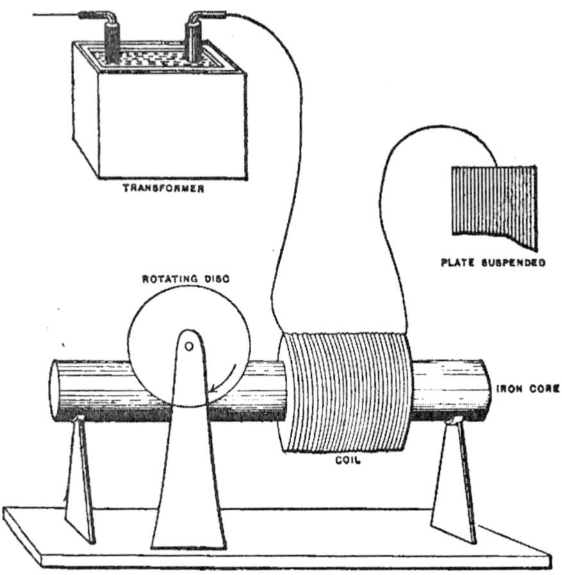

FIG. 17.—SINGLE WIRE AND "NO-WIRE" MOTOR.

connect the free end of the motor coil to an insulated body of some size. The experimenter's body is more than sufficient. If he touches the free terminal with an object held in the hand, a current passes through the coil and the copper disc is set in rotation. If an exhausted tube is put in series with the coil, the tube lights brilliantly, showing the passage of a strong current. Instead of the experimenter's body, a small metal sheet suspended on a cord may be used with the same result. In this case the plate acts as a condenser in series with the coil. It counteracts the self-induction of the latter and allows a strong current to pass. In such a combination, the greater the self-induction of the coil the smaller need be the plate, and this means that a lower frequency, or eventually a lower potential, is required to operate the motor. A single coil wound upon a core has a high self-induction; for this reason principally, this type of motor was chosen to perform the experiment. Were a secondary closed coil wound upon the core, it would tend to diminish the self-induction, and then it would be necessary to employ a much higher frequency and potential. Neither would be advisable, for a higher potential would endanger the insulation of the small primary coil, and a higher frequency would result in a materially diminished torque.

It should be remarked that when such a motor with a closed secondary is used, it is not at all easy to obtain rotation with excessive frequencies, as the secondary cuts off almost completely the lines of the primary—and this, of course, the more, the higher the frequency—and allows the passage of but a minute current. In such a case, unless the secondary is closed through a condenser, it is almost essential, in order to produce rotation, to make the primary and secondary coils overlap each other more or less.

But there is an additional feature of interest about this motor, namely, it is not necessary to have even a single connection between the motor and generator, except, perhaps, through the ground; for not only is an insulated plate capable of giving off energy into space, but it likewise capable of deriving it from an alternating electrostatic field, though in the latter case the available energy is much smaller. In this instance one of the motor terminals is connected to the insulated plate or body located within the alternating electrostatic field, and the other terminal preferably to the ground.

It is quite possible, however, that such "no-wire" motors, as they might be called, could be operated by conduction through the rarefied air at considerable distances. Alternate currents, especially of high frequencies, pass with astonishing freedom through even slightly rarefied gases. The upper strata of the air are rarefied. To reach a number of miles out into space requires the overcoming of difficulties of a merely mechanical nature. There is no doubt that with the enormous potentials obtainable by the use of high frequencies and oil insulation, luminous discharges might be passed through many miles of rarefied air, and that, by thus directing the energy of many hundreds or thousands of horse-power, motors or lamps might be operated at considerable distances from stationary sources. But such schemes are mentioned merely as possibilities. We shall have no need to transmit power at all. Ere many generations pass, our machinery will be driven by a power obtainable at any point of the universe. This idea is not novel. Men have been led to it long ago by instinct or reason; it has been expressed in many ways, and in many places, in the history of old and new. We find it in the delightful myth of Antheus [Antaeus], who derives power from the earth; we find it among the subtle speculations of one of your splendid mathematicians and in many hints and statements of thinkers of the present time. Throughout space there is energy. Is this energy static or kinetic? If static our hopes are in vain; if kinetic—and this we know it is, for certain—then it is a mere question of time when men will succeed in attaching their machinery to the very wheelwork of nature. Of all, living or dead, Crookes came nearest to doing it. His radiometer will turn in the light of day and in the darkness of the night; it will turn everywhere where there is heat, and heat is everywhere. But, unfortunately, this beautiful little machine, while it goes down to posterity as the most interesting, must likewise be put on record as the most inefficient machine ever invented!

The preceding experiment is only one of many equally interesting experiments which may be performed by thc use of only one wire with alternate currents of high potential and frequency. We may connect an insulated line to a source of such currents, we may pass an inappreciable current over the line, and on any point of the same we are able to obtain a heavy current, capable of fusing a thick copper wire. Or we may, by the help of some artifice, decompose a solution in any electrolytic cell by connecting only one pole of the cell to the line or source of energy. Or we may, by attaching to the line, or only bringing into its vicinity, light up an incandescent lamp, an exhausted tube, or a phosphorescent bulb.

However impracticable this plan of working may appear in many cases, it certainly seems practicable, and even recommendable, in the production of light. A perfected lamp would require but little energy, and if wires were used at all we ought to be able to supply that energy without a return wire.

It is now a fact that a body may be rendered incandescent or phosphorescent b) bringing it either in single contact or merely in the vicinity of a source of electric impulses of the proper character, and that in this manner a quantity of light sufficient to afford a practical illuminant may be produced. It is, therefore, to say the least, worth while to attempt to determine the best conditions and to invent the best appliances for attaining this object.

Some experiences have already been gained in this direction, and I will dwell on them briefly, in the hope that they might prove useful.

The heating of a conducting body inclosed in a bulb, and connected to a source of rapidly alternating electric impulses, is dependent on so many things of a different nature, that it would be difficult to give a generally applicable rule under which this maximum heating occurs. As regards the size of the vessel, I have lately found that at ordinary or only slightly differing atmospheric pressures, when air is a good insulator, and hence practically the same amount of energy by a certain potential and frequency is given off from the body, whether the bulb be small or large, the body is brought to a higher temperature if inclosed in a small bulb, because of the better confinement of heat in this case.

At lower pressures, when air becomes more or less conducting, or if the air be sufficiently warmed as to become conducting, the body is rendered more intensely incandescent in a large bulb, obviously because, under otherwise equal conditions of test, more energy may be given off from the body when the bulb is large.

At very high degrees of exhaustion, when the matter in the bulb becomes "radiant," a large bulb has still an advantage, but a comparatively slight one, over the small bulb.

Finally, at excessively high degrees of exhaustion, which cannot be reached except by the employment of special means, there seems to be, beyond a certain and rather small size of vessel, no perceptible difference in the heating.

These observations were the result of a number of experiments, of which one, showing the effect of the size of the bulb at a high degree of exhaustion may be described and shown here, as it presents a feature of interest. Three spherical bulbs of 2 inches, 3 inches and 4 inches diameter were taken, and in the centre of each was mounted an equal length of an ordinary incandescent lamp filament of uniform thickness. In each bulb the piece of filament was fastened to the leading-in wire of platinum, contained in a glass stem sealed in the bulb; care being taken, of course, to make everything as nearly alike as possible. On each glass stem in the inside of the bulb was slipped a highly polished tube made of aluminium sheet, which fitted the stem and was held on it by spring pressure. The function of this aluminium tube will be explained subsequently. In each bulb an equal length of filament protruded above the metal tube. It is sufficient to say now that under these conditions equal lengths of filament of the same thickness—in other words, bodies of equal bulk—were brought to incandescence. The three bulbs were sealed to a glass tube, which was connected to a Sprengel pump. When a high vacuum had been reached, the glass tube carrying the bulbs was sealed off. A current was then turned on successively on each bulb, and it was found that the filaments came to about the same brightness, and, if anything, the smallest bulb, which was placed midway between the two larger ones, may have been slightly brighter. This result was expected, for when either of the bulbs was connected to the coil the luminosity spread through the other two, hence the three bulbs constituted really one vessel. When all the three bulbs were connected in multiple arc to the coil, in the largest of them the filament glowed brightest, in the next smaller it was a little less bright, and in the smallest it only came to redness. The bulbs were then sealed off and separately tried. The brightness of the filaments was now such as mould have been expected on the supposition that the energy given off was proportionate to the surface of the bulb, this surface in each case representing one of the coatings of a condenser. Accordingly, there was less difference between the largest and the middle sited than between the latter and the smallest bulb.

An interesting observation was made in this experiment. The three bulbs were suspended from a straight bare wire connected to a terminal of the coil, the largest bulb being placed at the end of the wire, at some distance from it the smallest bulb, and an equal distance from the latter the middle-sized one. The carbons glowed then to both the larger bulbs about as expected, but the smallest did not get its share by far. This observation led me to exchange the position of the bulbs, and I then observed that whichever of the bulbs was in the middle it was by far less bright than it was in any other position. This mystifying result was, of course, found to be due to the electrostatic action between the bulbs. When they were placed at a considerable distance, or when they were attached to the corners of an equilateral triangle of copper wire, they glowed about in the order determined by their surfaces.

As to the shape of the vessel, it is also of some importance, especially at high degrees of exhaustion. Of all the possible constructions, it seems that a spherical globe with the refractory body mounted in its centre is the best to employ. In experience it has been demonstrated that in such a globe a refractory body of a given bulk is more easily brought to incandescence than when otherwise shaped bulbs are used. There is also an advantage in giving to the incandescent body the shape of a sphere, for self-evident reasons. In any case the body should be mounted in the centre, where the atoms rebounding from the glass collide. This object is best attained in the spherical bulb; but it is also attained in a cylindrical vessel with one or two straight filaments coinciding with its axis, and possibly also in parabolical or spherical bulbs with the refractory body or bodies placed in the focus or foci of the same; though the latter is not probable, as the electrified atoms should in all cases rebound normally from the surface they strike, unless the speed were excessive, in which case they *would* probably follow the general law of reflection. No matter what shape the vessel may have, if the exhaustion be low, a filament mounted in the globe is brought to the same degree of incandescence in all parts; but if the exhaustion be high and the bulb be spherical or pear-shaped, as usual, focal points form and the filament is heated to a higher degree at or near such points.

To illustrate the effect, I have here two small bulbs which are alike, only one is exhausted to a low and the other to a very high degree. When connected to the coil, the filament in the former glows uniformly throughout all its length; whereas in the latter, that portion of the filament which is in the centre of the bulb glows far more intensely than the rest. A curious point is that the phenomenon occurs even if two filament: are mounted in a bulb, each being connected to one terminal of the coil, and, what is still more curious, if they be very near together, provided the vacuum be very high. I noted in experiments with such bulbs that the filaments would give way usually at a certain point, and in the first trials I attributed it to a defect in the carbon. But when that phenomenon occurred many times in succession I recognized its real cause.

In order to bring a refractory body inclosed in a bulb to incandescence, it is desirable, on account of economy, that all the energy supplied to the bulb from the source should reach without lass the body to be heated; from there, and from nowhere else, it should be radiated. It is, of course, out of the question to reach this theoretical result, but it is possible by a proper construction of the illuminating device to approximate it more or less.

For many reasons, the refractory body is placed in the centre of the bulb and it is usually supported on a glass stem containing the leading-in wire. As the potential of this wire is alternated, the rarefied gas surrounding the stem is acted upon inductively, and the glass stem is violently bombarded and heated. In this manner by far the greater portion of the energy supplied to the bulb—especially when exceedingly high frequencies are used—may be lost for the purpose contemplated. To obviate this loss, or at least to reduce it to a minimum,

I usually screen the rarefied gas surrounding the stem from the inductive action of the leading-in wire by providing; the stem with a tube or coating of conducting material. It seems beyond doubt that the best among metals to employ for this purpose is aluminium, on account of its many remarkable properties. Its only fault is that it is easily fusible and, therefore, its distance from the incandescing: body should be properly estimated. Usually, a thin tube, of a diameter somewhat smaller than that of the glass stem, is made of the finest aluminium sheet, and slipped on the stem. The tube is conveniently prepared by wrapping around a rod fastened in a lathe a piece of aluminium sheet of the proper size, grasping the sheet firmly with clean chamois leather or blotting paper, and spinning the rod very fast. The sheet is wound tightly around the rod, and a highly polished tube of one or three layers of the sheet is obtained. When slipped on the stem, the pressure is generally sufficient to prevent it from slipping off, but, for safety, the lower edge of the sheet may be turned inside. The upper inside corner of the sheet—that is, the one which is nearest to the refractory incandescent body—should be cut out diagonally, as it often happens that, in consequence of the intense heat, this corner turns toward the inside and comes very near to, or in contact with, the wire, or filament, supporting the refractory body. The greater part of the energy supplied to the bulb is then used up in heating the metal tube, and the bulb is rendered useless for the purpose. The aluminium sheet should project above the glass stem more or less—one inch or so—or else, if the glass be too close to the incandescing body, it may be strongly heated and become more or less conducting, whereupon it may be ruptured, or may, by its conductivity, establish a good electrical connection between the metal tube and the leadinq-in wire, in which case, again, most of the energy will be lost in heating the former. Perhaps the best way is to make the top of the glass tube for about an inch, of a much smaller diameter. To still further reduce the danger arising from the heating of the glass stem, and also with the view of preventing an electrical connection between the metal tube and the electrode, I preferably wrap; the stem with several layers of thin mica which extends at least as far as the metal tube. In some bulbs I have also used an outside insulating cover.

The preceding remarks are only made to aid the experimenter in the first trials, for the difficulties which he encounters he may soon find means to overcome in his own way.

To illustrate the effect of the screen, and the advantage of using it, I have here two bulbs of the same size, with their stems, leading-in wires and incandescent lamp filaments tied to the latter, as nearly alike as possible. The stem of one bulb is provided with an aluminium tube, the stem of the other has none. Originally the two bulbs were joined by a tube which was connected to a Sprengel pump. When a high vacuum had been reached, first the connecting tube, and then the bulbs, were sealed off; they are therefore of the same degree of exhaustion. When they are separately connected to the coil giving a certain potential, the carbon filament in the bulb provided with the aluminium screen in rendered highly incandescent, while the filament in the other bulb may, with the same potential, not even come to redness, although in reality the latter bulb takes generally more energy than the former. When they are both connected together to the terminal, the difference is even more apparent, showing the importance of the screening. The metal tube placed in the stem containing the leading-in wire performs really two distinct functions: First, it acts more or less as an electrostatic screen, thus economizing the energy supplied to the bulb; and, second, to whatever extent it may fail to act electrostatically, it acts mechanically, preventing the bombardment, and consequently intense heating and possible deterioration of the slender support of the refractory incandescent body, or of the glass stem containing the leading-in wire. I say *slender* support, for it is evident that in order to confine the heat more completely to the incandescing body its support should be very thin, so as to carry away the smallest possible amount of heat by conduction. Of all the supports used I have found an ordinary incandescent lamp filament to be the best, principally because among conductors it can withstand the highest degrees of heat.

The effectiveness of the metal tube as an electrostatic screen depends largely on the degree of exhaustion.

At excessively high degrees of exhaustion—which are reached by using great care and special means in connection with the Sprengel pump—when the matter in the globe is in the ultra-radiant state, it acts most perfectly. The shadow of the upper edge of the tube is then sharply defined upon the bulb.

At a somewhat lower degree of exhaustion, which is about the ordinary "non-striking" vacuum, and generally as long as the matter moves predominantly in straight lines, the screen still does well. In elucidation of the preceding remark it is necessary to state that what is a "non-striking" vacuum for a coil operated, as ordinarily, by impulses, or currents, of low frequency, is not, by far, so when the coil is operated by currents of very high frequency. In such case the discharge may pass with great freedom through the rarefied gas through which a low-frequency discharge may not pass, even though the potential be much higher. At ordinary atmospheric pressures just the reverse rule holds good: the higher the frequency, the less the spark discharge is able to jump between the terminals, especially if they are knobs or spheres of some size.

Finally, at very low degrees of exhaustion, when the gas is well conducting, the metal tube not only does not act as an electrostatic screen, but even is a drawback, aiding to a considerable extent the dissipation of the energy laterally from the leading-in wire. This, of course, is to be expected. In this case, namely, the metal tube is in good electrical connection with -the leading-in wire, and most of the bombardment is directed upon the tube. As long as the electrical connection is not good, the conducting tube is always of some advantage for although it may not greatly economize energy, still it protects the support of the refractory button, and is a means for concentrating more energy upon the same.

To whatever extent the aluminium tube performs the function of a screen, its usefulness is therefore limited to very high degrees of exhaustion when it is insulated from the electrode—that is, when the gas as a whole is non-conducting, and the molecules, or atoms, act as independent carriers of electric charges.

In addition to acting as a more or less effective screen, in the true meaning of the word, the conducting tube or coating may also act, by reason of its conductivity, as a sort of equalizer or dampener of the bombardment against the stem. To be explicit, I assume the action as follows: Suppose a rhythmical bombardment to occur against the conducting tube by reason of its imperfect action as a screen, it certainly must happen that some molecules, or atoms, strike the tube sooner than others. Those which come first in contact with it give up their superfluous charge, and the tube is electrified, the electrification instantly spreading over its surface. But this must diminish, the energy lost in the bombardment for two reasons: first, the charge given up by the atoms spreads over a great area, and hence the electric density at any point is small, and the atoms are rebelled with less energy than they would be if they would strike against a good insulator; secondly, as the tube is electrified by the atoms which first come in contact with it, the progress of the following atoms against the tube is more or less checked by, the repulsion which the electrified tube must exert upon the similarly electrified atoms. This repulsion may perhaps be sufficient to prevent a large portion of the atoms from striking the tube, but at any rate it must diminish the energy of their impact. It is clear that when the exhaustion is very low, and the rarefied gas well conducting, neither of the above effects can occur, and, on the other hand, the fewer the atoms, with the greater freedom they move; in other words, the higher the degree of exhaustion, up to a limit, the more telling will be both the effects:

What I have just said may afford an explanation of the phenomenon observed by Prof. Crookes, namely, that a discharge through a bulb is established with much greater facility when an insulator than when a conductor is present in the same. In my opinion, the conductor acts as a dampener of the motion of the atoms in the two ways pointed out; hence, to cause a visible discharge to pass through the bulb, a much higher potential is needed if a conductor, especially of many surfaces, be present.

For the sake of clearness of some of the remarks before made, I must now refer to Figs. 18, 19, and 20, which illustrate various arrangements with a type of bulb most generally used.

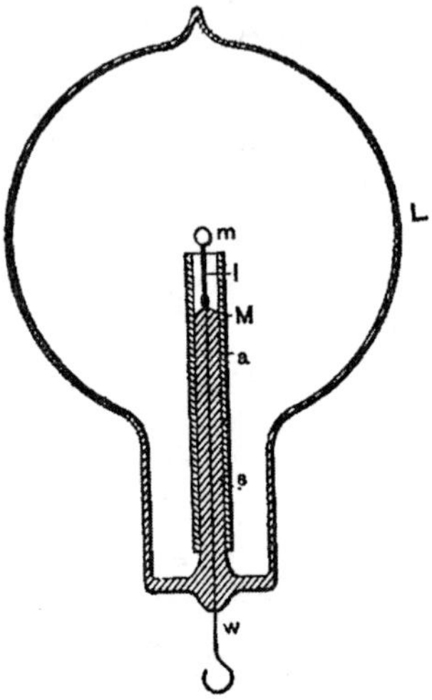

FIG. 18.—BULB WITH MICA TUBE AND ALUMINIUM SCREEN.

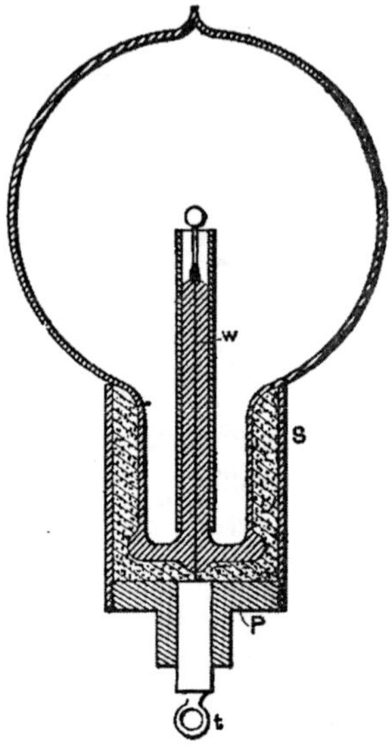

FIG. 19.—IMPROVED BULB WITH SOCKET AND SCREEN.

Fig. 18 is a section though a spherical bulb L, with the glass stem *s*, containing the leading-in wire *w*, which has a lamp filament *l* fastened to it, serving to support the refractory button *m* in the centre. M is a sheet of thin mica wound in several layers around the stem *s*, and *a* is the aluminium tube.

Fig. 19 illustrates such a bulb in a somewhat more advanced stage of perfection. A metallic tube S is fastened by means of some cement to the neck of the tube. In the tube is screwed a plug P, of insulating material, in the centre of which is fastened a metallic terminal *t*, for the connection to the lead-in wire *w*. This terminal must be well insulated from the metal tube S, therefore, if the cement used is conducting and most generally it is sufficiently so—the space between the plug P and the neck of the bulb should be filled with some good insulating material, as mica powder.

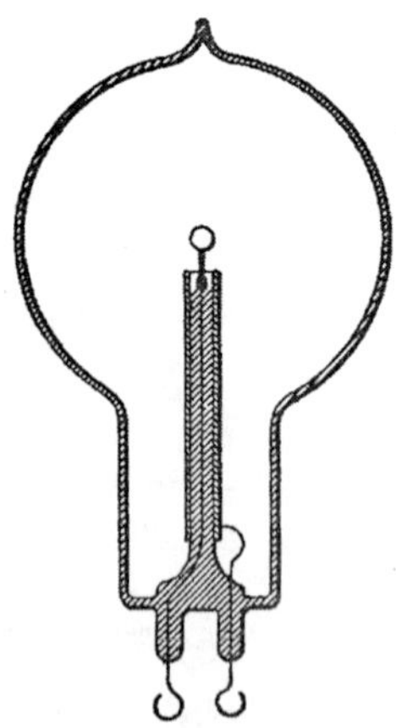

FIG. 20.–BULB FOR EXPERIMENTS WITH CONDUCTING TUBE.

Fig. 20 shows a bulb made for experimental purposes. In this bulb the aluminium tube is provided with an external connection, which serves to investigate the effect of the tube under various conditions. It is referred to chiefly to suggest a line of experiment followed.

Since the bombardment against the stem containing the leading-in wire is due to the inductive action of the latter upon the rarefied gas, it is of advantage to reduce this action as far as practicable by employing a very thin wire, surrounded by a very thick insulation of glass or other material, and by making the wire passing through the rarefied gas as short as practicable. To combine these features I employ a large tube T (Fig. 21), which protrudes into the bulb to some distance, and carries on the top a very short glass stem *s*, into which is sealed the leading-in wire *w*, and I protect the top of the glass stem against the heat by a small, aluminium tube *a* and a layer of mica underneath the same, as usual. The wire *w*, passing through the large tube to the outside of the bulb, should be well insulated—with a glass tube, for instance—and the space between ought to be filled out with some excellent insulator. Among many insulating powders I have tried, I have found that mica powder is the best to employ. If this precaution is not taken, the tube T, protruding into the bulb, will surely be cracked in consequence of the heating by the brushes which are apt to form in the upper part of the tube, near the exhausted globe, especially if the vacuum be excellent, and therefore the potential necessary to operate the lamp be very high.

Fig. 22 illustrates a similar arrangement, with a large tube T protruding into the part of the bulb containing the refractory button *m*. In this case the wire leading from the outside into the bulb is omitted, the energy required being supplied through condenser coatings C C. The insulating packing P should in this construction be tightly fitting to the glass, and rather wide, or otherwise the discharge might avoid passing through the wire *w*, which connects the inside condenser coating to the incandescent button *m*.

The molecular bombardment against the glass stem in the bulb is a source of great trouble. As illustration I will cite a phenomenon only too frequently and unwillingly observed. A bulb, preferably a large one, may be taken, and a good conducting body, such as a piece of carbon, may be mounted in it upon a platinum wire sealed in the glass stem. The bulb may be exhausted to a fairly high degree, nearly to the point when phosphorescence begins to appear. When the bulb is connected with the coil, the piece of carbon, if small, may become highly incandescent at first, but its brightness immediately diminishes, and then the discharge may break through the glass somewhere in the middle of the stem, in the form of bright sparks, in spite of the fact that the platinum wire is in good electrical connection with the rarefied gas through the piece of carbon or metal at the top. The first sparks are singularly bright, recalling those drawn from a clear surface of mercury. But, as they heat the glass rapidly, they, of course, lose their brightness, and cease when the glass at the ruptured place becomes incandescent, or generally sufficiently hot to conduct. When

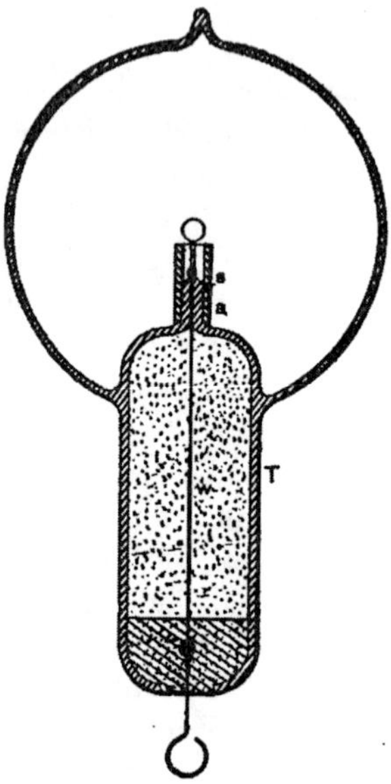

FIG. 21.—IMPROVED BULB WITH NON-CONDUCTING BUTTON.

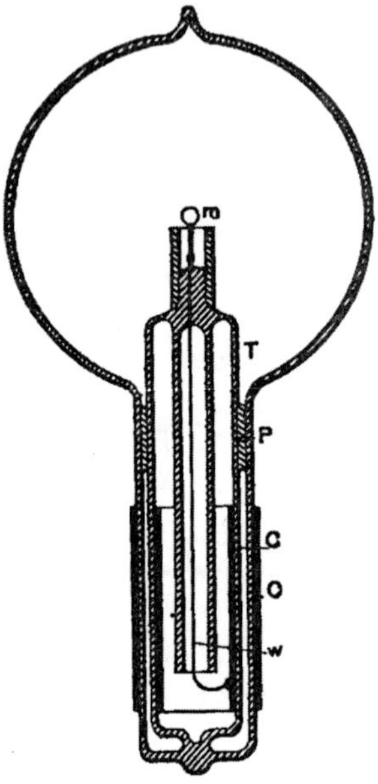

FIG. 22.—TYPE OF BULB WITHOUT LEADING-IN WIRE.

observed for the first time the phenomenon must appear very curious, and shows in a striking manner how radically different alternate currents, or impulses, of high frequency behave, as compared with steady currents, or currents of low frequency. With such currents—namely, the latter—the phenomenon would of course not occur. When frequencies such as are obtained by mechanical means are used, I think that the rupture of the glass is more or less the consequence of the bombardment, which warms it up and impairs its insulating power; but with frequencies obtainable with condensers I have no doubt that the glass may give way without previous heating. Although this appears most singular at first, it is in reality what we might expect to occur. The energy supplied to the wire leading into the bulb is given off partly by direct action through the carbon button, and party by inductive action through the glass surrounding the wire. The case is thus analogous to that in

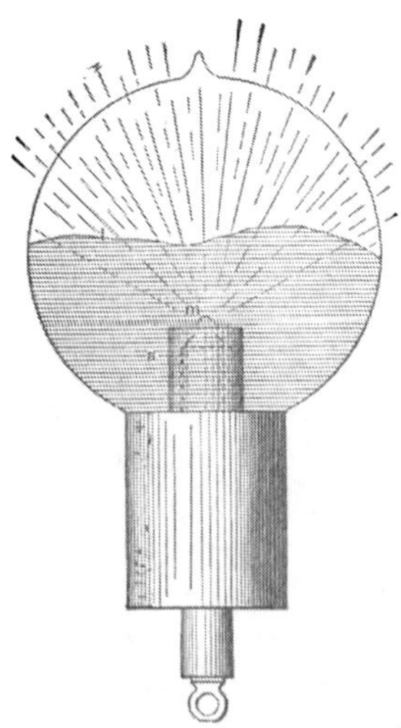

FIG. 23.—EFFECT PRODUCED BY A RUBY DROP.

which a condenser shunted by a conductor of low resistance is connected to a source of alternating currents. As long as the frequencies are low, the conductor gets the most, and the condenser is perfectly safe; but when the frequency becomes excessive, the *role* of the conductor may become quite insignificant. In the latter case the difference of potential at the terminals of the condenser may become so great as to rupture the dielectric, notwithstanding the fact that the terminals are joined by a conductor of low resistance.

It is, of course, not necessary, when it is desired to produce the incandescence of a body inclosed in a bulb by means of these currents, that the body should be a conductor, for even a perfect non-conductor may be quite as readily heated. For this purpose it is sufficient to surround a conducting electrode with a non-conducting material, as, for instance, in the bulb described before in Fig. 21, in which a thin incandescent lamp filament is coated with a non-conductor, and supports a button of the same material on the top. At the start the bombardment goes on by inductive action through the non-conductor, until the same is sufficiently heated to become conducting, then the bombardment continues in the ordinary way.

A different arrangement used in some of the bulbs constructed is illustrated in Fig. 23. In this instance a non-conductor *m* is mounted in a piece of common arc light carbon so as to project some small distance above the latter. The carbon piece is connected to the leading-in wire passing through a glass stem, which is wrapped with several layers of mica. An aluminium tube a is employed as usual for screening. It is so arranged that it reaches very nearly as high as the carbon and only the non-conductor m projects a little above it. The bombardment goes at first against the upper surface of carbon, the lower parts being protected by the aluminium tube. As soon, however, as the non-conductor m is heated it is rendered good conducting, and then it becomes the centre of the bombardment, being most exposed to the same.

I have also constructed during these experiments many such single-wire bulbs with or without internal electrode, in which the radiant matter was projected against, or focused upon, the body to be rendered incandescent. Fig. 24 illustrates one of the bulbs used. It consists of a spherical globe L, provided with a long neck *n*, on the top, for increasing the action in some cases by the application of an external conducting coating. The globe L is blown out on the bottom into a very small bulb *b*, which serves to hold it firmly in a socket S of insulating material into which it is cemented. A fine lamp filament *f*, supported on a wire *w*, passes through the centre of filament is rendered incandescent In the middle portion, where the bombardment proceeding from the lower inside surface of the globe is most intense. The lower portion of the globe, as far as the socket S reaches, is rendered conducting, either by g tinfoil coating or otherwise, and the external electrode is connected to a terminal of the coil.

The arrangement diagrammatically indicated in Fig. 24 was found to be an inferior one when it was desired to render incandescent a filament or button supported in the centre of the globe, but it was convenient when the object was to excite phosphorescence.

In many experiments in which bodies of a different kind were mounted in the bulb as, for instance, indicated in Fig. 23, some observations of interest were made.

It was found, among other things, that in such cases, no matter where the bombardment began, just as soon as a high temperature was reached there was generally one of the bodies which seemed to take most of the bombardment upon itself, the other, or others, being thereby relieved. This quality appeared to depend principally on the point of fusion, and on the facility with which the body was "evaporated," or, generally speaking, disintegrated—meaning by the latter term not only the throwing off of atoms, but likewise of larger lumps. The observation made was in accordance with generally accepted notions. In a highly exhausted bulb electricity is carried off from the electrode by independent carriers, which are partly the atoms, or molecules, of the residual atmosphere, and partly the atoms, molecules, or lumps thrown off from the electrode. If the electrode is composed of bodies of different character, and if one of these is more easily disintegrated than the others, most of the electricity supplied is carried off from that body, which is then brought to a higher temperature than the others, and this the more, as upon an increase of the temperature the body is still more easily disintegrated.

It seems to me quite probable that a similar process takes place in the bulb even with a homogenous electrode, and I think it to be the principal cause of the disintegration. There is bound to be some irregularity, even if the surface is highly polished, which, of course, is impossible with most of the refractory bodies employed as electrodes. Assume that a point of the electrode gets hotter, instantly most of the discharge passes through that point, and a minute patch is probably fused and evaporated. It is now possible that in consequence of the violent disintegration the spot attacked sinks in temperature, or that a counter force is created, as in an arc; at any rate, the local tearing off meets with the limitations incident to the experiment, where upon the same process occurs on another place. To the eye the electrode appears uniformly brilliant, but there are upon it points constantly shifting and wandering around, of a temperature far above the mean, and this materially hastens the process of deterioration. That some such thing occurs, at least when the electrode is at a lower temperature, sufficient experimental evidence can be obtained in the following manner: Exhaust a bulb to a very high degree, so that with a fairly high potential the discharge cannot pass—that is, not a *luminous* one, for a weak invisible discharge occurs always, in all probability. Now raise slowly and carefully the potential, leaving the primary current on no mote than for an instant. At a certain point, two, three, or half a dozen phosphorescent spots mill appear on the globe. These places of the glass are evidently more violently bombarded than others, this being due to the unevenly distributed electric density, necessitated, of course, by sharp projections, or, generally speaking, irregularities of the electrode. But the luminous patches are constantly changing in position, which is especially well observable if one manages to produce very few, and this indicates that the configuration of the electrode is rapidly changing.

From experiences of this kind I am led to infer that, in order to be most durable, the refractory button in the bulb should be in the form of a sphere with a highly polished surface. Such a small sphere could be manufactured from a diamond or some other crystal, but a better way would be to fuse, by the employment of extreme degrees of temperature, some oxide—as, for instance, zirconia—into a small drop, and then keep it in the bulb at a temperature somewhat below its point of fusion.

Interesting and useful results can no doubt be reached in the direction of extreme degrees of heat. How can such high temperatures be arrived at? How are the highest degrees of heat reached in nature? By the impact of stars, by high speeds and collisions. In a collision any rate of heat generation may be attained. In a chemical process we are limited. When oxygen and hydrogen combine, they fall, metaphorically speaking, from a definite height. We cannot go very far with a blast, nor by confining heat in a furnace, but in an exhausted bulb we can concentrate any amount of energy upon a minute button. Leaving practicability out of consideration, this, then, would be the means which, in my opinion, would enable us to reach the highest temperature. But a great difficulty when proceeding in this way is encountered, namely, in most cases the body is carried off before it can fuse and form a drop. This difficulty exists principally with an oxide such as zirconia, because it cannot be compressed in so hard a cake that it would not be carried off quickly. I endeavored repeatedly to fuse zirconia, placing it in a cup or arc light carbon as indicated in Fig. 23. It glowed with a most intense light, and the stream of the particles projected out of the carbon cup was of a vivid white; but whether it was compressed in a cake or made into a paste with carbon, it was carried off before it could be fused. The carbon cup containing the zirconia had to be mounted very low in the neck of a large bulb, as the heating of the glass by the projected particles of the oxide was so rapid that in the first trial the bulb was cracked almost in an instant when the current was turned on. The heating of the glass by the projected particles was found to be always greater when the carbon cup contained a body which was rapidly carried off—I presume because in such cases, with the same potential, higher speeds were reached, and also because, per unit of time, more matter was projected—that is, more particles would strike the glass.

The before mentioned difficulty did not exist, however, when the body mounted in the carbon cup offered great resistance to deterioration. For instance, when an oxide was first fused in an oxygen blast and then mounted in the bulb, it melted very readily into a drop.

Generally during the process of fusion magnificent light effects were noted, of which it would be difficult to give an adequate idea. Fig. 23 is intended to illustrate the effect observed with a ruby drop. At first one may see a narrow funnel of white light projected against the top of the globe, where it produces an irregularly outlined phosphorescent patch. When the point of the ruby fuses the phosphorescence becomes very powerful; but as the atoms are projected with much greater speed from the surface of the drop, soon the glass gets hot and "tired," and now only the outer edge of the patch glows. In this manner an intensely phosphorescent, sharply defined line, corresponding to the outline of the drop, is produced, which spreads slowly: over the globe as the drop gets larger. When the mass begins to boil, small bubbles and cavities are formed, which cause dark colored spots to sweep across the globe. The bulb may be turned downward without fear of the drop falling off, as the mass possesses considerable viscosity.

I may mention here another feature of some interest, which I believe to have noted in the course of these experiments, though the observations do not amount to a certitude. It *appeared* that under the molecular impact caused by the rapidly alternating potential the body was fused and maintained in that state at a lower temperature in a highly exhausted bulb than was the case at normal pressure and application of heat in the ordinary way—that is, at least, judging from the quantity of the light emitted. One of the experiments performed may be mentioned here by way of illustration. A small piece of pumice stone was stuck on a platinum wire, and first melted to it in a gas burner. The wire was next placed between two pieces of charcoal and a burner applied so as to produce an intense heat, sufficient to melt down the pumice stone into a small glass-like button. The platinum wire had to be taken of sufficient thickness to prevent its melting in the fire. While in the charcoal fire, or when held in a burner to get a better idea of the degree of heat, the button glowed with great brilliancy. The wire with the button was then mounted in a bulb, and upon exhausting the same to a high degree, the current was turned on slowly so as to prevent the cracking of the button. The button was heated to the point of fusion, and when it melted it did not, apparently, glow with the same brilliancy as before, and this would indicate a lower temperature. Leaving out of consideration the observer's possible, and even probable, error, the question is, can a body under these conditions be brought from a solid to a liquid state with evolution of *less* light?

When the potential of a body is rapidly alternated it is certain that the structure is jarred. When the potential is very high, although the vibrations may be few—say 20,000 per second—the effect upon the structure may be considerable. Suppose, for example, that a ruby is melted into a drop by a steady application of energy. When it forms a drop it will emit visible and invisible waves, which will be in a definite ratio, and to the eye the drop will appear to be of a certain brilliancy. Next, suppose we diminish to any degree we choose the energy steadily supplied, and, instead, supply energy which rises and falls according to a certain law. Now, when the drop is formed, there will be emitted from it three different kinds of vibrations—the ordinary visible, and two kinds of invisible waves: that is, the ordinary dark waves of all lengths, and, in addition, waves of a well-defined character. The latter would not exist by a steady supply of the energy; still they help to jar and loosen the structure. If this really be the case, then the ruby drop will emit relatively less visible and more invisible waves than before. Thus it would seem that when a platinum wire, for instance, is fused by currents alternating with extreme rapidity, it emits at the point of fusion less light and more invisible radiation than it does when melted by a steady current, though the total energy used up in the process of fusion is the same in both cases, Or, to cite another example, a lamp filament is not capable of withstanding as long with currents of extreme frequency as it does with steady currents, assuming that it be worked at the same luminous intensity. This means that for rapidly alternating currents the filament should be shorter and thicker. The higher the frequency—that is, the greater the departure from the steady flow—the worse it would be for the filament. But if the truth of this remark were demonstrated, it would be erroneous to conclude that such a refractory button as used in these bulbs would be deteriorated quicker by currents of extremely high frequency than by steady or low frequency currents. From experience I may say that just the opposite holds good: the button withstands the bombardment better with currents of very high frequency. But this is due to the fact that a high frequency discharge passes through a rarefied gas with much greater freedom than a steady or low frequency discharge, and this will say that with the former we can work with a lower potential or with a less violent impact. As long, then, as the gas is of no consequence, a steady or low frequency current is better; but as soon as the action of the gas is desired and important, high frequencies are preferable.

In the course of these experiments a great many trials were made with all kinds of carbon buttons. Electrodes made of ordinary carbon buttons were decidedly more durable when the buttons were obtained by the application of enormous pressure. Electrodes prepared by depositing carbon in well known ways did not show up well; they blackened the globe very quickly. From many experiences I conclude that lamp filaments obtained in this manner can be advantageously used only with low potentials and low frequency currents. Some kinds of carbon withstand so well that, in order to bring them to the point of fusion, it is necessary to employ very small buttons. In this case the observation is rendered very difficult on account of the intense heat produced.

Nevertheless there can be no doubt that all kinds of carbon are fused under the molecular bombardment, but the liquid state must be one of great instability. Of all the bodies tried there were two which withstood best—diamond and carborundum. These two showed up about equally, but the latter was preferable, for many reasons. As it is more than likely that this body is not yet generally known, I will venture to call your attention to it.

It has been recently produced by Mr. E. G. Acheson, of Monongahela City, Pa., U. S. A. It is intended to replace ordinary diamond powder for polishing precious stones, etc., and I have been informed that it accomplishes this object quite successfully. I do not know why the name "carborundum" has been given to it, unless there is something in the process of its manufacture which justifies this selection. Through the kindness of the inventor, I obtained a short while ago some samples which I desired to test in regard to their qualities of phosphorescence and capability of withstanding high degrees of heat.

Carborundum can be obtained in two forms—in the form of "crystals" and of powder. The former appear to the naked eye dark colored, but are very brilliant; the latter is of nearly the same color as ordinary diamond powder, but very much finer. When viewed under a microscope the samples of crystals given to me did not appear to have any definite form, but rather resembled pieces of broken up egg coal of fine quality. The majority were opaque, but there were some which were transparent and colored. The crystals are a kind of carbon containing some impurities; they are extremely hard, and withstand for a long time even an oxygen blast. When the blast is directed against them they at first form a cake of some compactness, probably in consequence of the fusion of impurities they contain. The mass withstands for a very long time the blast without further fusion; but a slow carrying off, or burning, occurs, and, finally, a small quantity of a glass-like residue is left, which, I suppose, is melted alumina. When compressed strongly they conduct very well, but not as well as ordinary carbon. The powder, which is obtained from the crystals in some way, is practically non-conducting. It affords a magnificent polishing material for stones.

The time has been too short to make a satisfactory study of the properties of this product, but enough experience has been gained in a few weeks I have experimented upon it to say that it does possess some remarkable properties in many respects. It withstands excessively high degrees of heat, it is little deteriorated by molecular bombardment, and it does not blacken the globe as ordinary carbon does. The only difficulty which I have found in its use in connection with these experiments was to find some binding material which would resist the heat and the effect of the bombardment as successfully as carborundum itself does.

I have here a number of bulbs which I have provided with buttons of carborundum. To make such a button of carborundum crystals I proceed in the following manner: I take an ordinary lamp filament and dip its point in tar, or some other thick substance or paint which may be readily carbonized. I next pass the point of the filament through the crystals, and then hold it vertically over a hot plate. The tar softens and forms a drop on the point of the filament, the crystals adhering to the surface of the drop. By regulating the distance from the plate the tar is slowly dried out and the button becomes solid. I then once more dip the button in tar and hold it again over a plate until the tar is evaporated, leaving only a hard mass which firmly binds the crystals. When a larger button is required I repeat the process several times, and I generally also cover the filament a certain distance below the button with crystals. The button being mounted in a bulb, when a good vacuum has been reached, first a weak and then a strong discharge is passed through the bulb to carbonize the tar and expel all gases, and later it is brought to a very intense incandescence.

When the powder is used I have found it best to proceed as follows: I make a thick paint of carborundum and tar, and pass a lamp filament through the paint. Taking then most of the paint off by rubbing the filament against a piece of chamois leather, I hold it over a hot plate until the tar evaporates and the coating becomes firm. I repeat this process as many times as it is necessary to obtain a certain thickness of coating. On the point of the coated filament I form a button in the same manner.

There is no doubt that such a button—properly prepared under great pressure—of carborundum, especially of powder of the best quality, will withstand the effect of the bombardment fully as well as anything we know. The difficulty is that the binding material gives way, and the carborundum is slowly thrown off after some time. As it does not seem to blacken the globe in the least, it might be found useful for coating the filaments of ordinary Incandescent lamps, and I think that it is even possible to produce thin threads or sticks of carborundum which will replace the ordinary filaments in an incandescent lamp. A carborundum coating seems to be more durable than other coatings, not only because the carborundum can withstand high degrees of heat, but also because it seems to unite with the carbon better than any other material I have tried. A coating of zirconia or any other oxide, for instance, is far more quickly destroyed. I prepared buttons of diamond dust in the same manner as of carborundum, and these came in durability nearest to those prepared of carborundum, but the binding paste gave way much more quickly in the diamond buttons: this, however, I attributed to the site and irregularity of the grains of the diamond.

It was of interest to find whether carborundum possesses the quality of phosphorescence. One is, of course, prepared to encounter two difficulties: first, as regards the rough product, the "crystals," they are good conducting, and it is a fact that conductors do not phosphoresce; second, the powder, being exceedingly fine, would not be apt to exhibit very prominently this quality, since we know that when crystals, even such as diamond or ruby, are finely powdered, they lose the property of phosphorescence to a considerable degree.

The question presents itself here, can a conductor phosphoresce? What is there in such a body as a metal, for instance, that would deprive it of the quality of phosphorescence, unless it is that property which characterizes it as a conductor? For it is a fact that most of the phosphorescent bodies lose that quality when they are sufficiently heated to become more or less conducting. Then, if a metal be in a large measure, or perhaps entirely deprived of that property, it should be capable of phosphorescence. Therefore it is quite possible that at some extremely high frequency, when behaving practically as a non-conductor, a metal of any other conductor might exhibit the quality of phosphorescence, even though it be entirely incapable of phosphorescing under the impact of a low-frequency discharge. There is, however, another possible way how a conductor might at least *appear* to phosphoresce.

Considerable doubt still exists as to what really is phosphorescence, and as to whether the various phenomena comprised under this head are due to the same causes. Suppose that in an exhausted bulb, under the molecular impact, the surface of a piece of metal or other conductor is rendered strongly luminous, but at the same time it is found that it remains comparatively cool, would not this luminosity be called phosphorescence? Now such a result, theoretically at least, is possible, for it is a mere question of potential of speed. Assume the potential of the electrode, and consequently the speed of the projected atoms, to be sufficiently high, the surface of the metal piece against which the atoms are projected would be rendered highly incandescent, since the process of heat generation would be incompatibly faster than that of radiating or conducting away from the surface of the collision. In the eye of the observer a single impact of the atoms would cause an instantaneous flash, but if the impact were repeated with sufficient rapidity they would produce a continuous impression upon his retina. To him then the surface of the metal would appear continuously incandescent and of constant luminous intensity, while in reality the light would be either intermittent or at least changing periodically in intensity. The metal piece would rise in temperature until equilibrium was attained—that is, until the energy continuously radiated would equal that intermittently supplied. But the supplied energy might under such conditions not be sufficient to bring the body to any more than a very moderate mean temperature, especially if the frequency of the atomic impacts be very low—just enough that the fluctuation of the intensity of the light emitted could not be detected by the eye. The body would now, owing to the manner in which the energy is supplied, emit a strong light, and yet be at a comparatively very low mean temperature. How could the observer call the luminosity thus produced? Even if the analysis of the light would teach him something definite, still he would probably rank it under the phenomena of phosphorescence. It is conceivable that in such a way both conducting and nonconducting bodies may be maintained at a certain-luminous intensity, but the energy required would very greatly vary with the nature and properties of the bodies.

These and some foregoing remarks of a speculative nature were made merely to bring out curious features of alternate currents or electric impulses. By their help we may cause a body to emit *more* light, while at a certain mean temperature, than it would emit if brought to that temperature by a steady supply; and, again, we may bring a body to the point of fusion, and cause it to emit *less* light than when fused by the application of energy in ordinary ways. It all depends on how we supply the energy, and what kind of vibrations we set up: in one case the vibrations are more, in the other less, adapted to affect our sense of vision.

Some effects, which I had not observed before, obtained with carborundum in the first trials, I attributed to phosphorescence, but in subsequent experiments it appeared that it was devoid of that quality. The crystals possess a noteworthy feature. In a bulb provided with a single electrode in the shape of a small circular metal disc, for instance, at a certain degree of exhaustion the electrode is covered with a milky film, which is separated by a dark space from the glow filling the bulb. When the metal disc is covered with carborundum crystals, the film is far more intense, and snow-white. This I found later to be merely an effect of the bright surface of the crystals, for when an aluminium electrode was highly polished it exhibited more or less the same phenomenon. I made a number of experiments with the samples of crystals obtained, principally because it would have been of special interest to find that they are capable of phosphorescence, on account of their being conducting. I could not produce phosphorescence distinctly, but I must remark that a decisive opinion cannot be formed until other experimenters have gone over the same ground.

The powder behaved in some experiments as though it contained alumina, but it did not exhibit with sufficient distinctness the red of the latter. Its dead color brightens considerably under the molecular impact, but I am now convinced it does not phosphoresce. Still, the tests with the powder are not conducive, because powdered carborundum probably does not behave like a phosphorescent sulphide, for example, which could be finely powdered without impairing the phosphorescence, but rather like powdered ruby or diamond, and therefore it would be necessary, in order to make a decisive test, to obtain it in a large lump and polish up the surface.

If the carborundum proves useful in connection with these and similar experiments, its chief value will be found in the production of coatings, thin conductors, buttons, or other electrodes capable of withstanding extremely high degrees of heat.

The production of a small electrode capable of withstanding enormous temperatures I regard as of the greatest importance in the manufacture of light. It would enable us to obtain, by means of currents of very high frequencies, certainly 20 times, if not more, the quantity of light which is obtained in the present incandescent lamp by the same expenditure of energy. This estimate may appeal- to many exaggerated, but in reality I think it is far from being so. As this statement might be misunderstood I think it necessary to expose clearly the problem with which in this line of work we are confronted, and the manner in which, in my opinion, a solution will be arrived at.

Any one who begins a study of the problem will be apt to think that what is wanted in a lamp with an electrode is a very high degree of incandescence of the electrode. There he will be mistaken. The high incandescence of the button is a necessary evil, but what is really wanted is the high incandescence of the gas surrounding thee button. In other words, the problem in such a lamp is to bring a mass of gas to the highest possible incandescence. The higher the incandescence, the quicker the mean vibration, the greater is the economy of the light production. But to maintain a mass of gas at a high degree of incandescence in a glass vessel, it will always be necessary to keep the incandescent mass away from the glass; that is, to confine it as much as possible to the central portion of the globe.

In one of the experiments this evening a brush was produced at the end of a wire. This brush was a flame, a source of heat and light. It did not emit much perceptible heat, nor did it glow with an intense light; but is it the less a flame because it does not scorch my hand? Is it the less a flame because it does not hurt my eye by its brilliancy? The problem is precisely to produce in the bulb such a flame, much smaller in site, but incomparably more powerful. Were there means at hand for producing electric impulses of a sufficiently high frequency, and for transmitting them, the bulb could be done away with, unless it were used to protect the electrode, or to economize the energy by confining the heat. But as such means are not at disposal, it becomes necessary to place The terminal in a bulb and rarefy the air in the same. This is done merely to enable the apparatus to perform the work which it is not capable of performing at ordinary air pressure. In the bulb we are able to intensify the action to any degree—so far that the brush emits a powerful light.

The intensity of the light emitted depends principally on the frequency and potential of the impulses, and on the electric density on the surface of the electrode. It is of the greatest importance to employ the smallest possible button, in order to push the density very far. Under the violent impact of the molecules of the gas surrounding it, the small electrode is of course brought to an extremely high temperature, but around it is a mass of highly incandescent gas, a flame photosphere, many hundred times the volume of the electrode. With a diamond, carborundum or zircon button the photosphere can be as much as one thousand times the volume of the button. Without much reflecting one would think that in pushing so far the incandescence of the electrode it would be instantly volatilized. But after a careful consideration he would find that, theoretically, it should not occur, and in this fact—which, however, is experimentally demonstrated—lies principally the future value of such a lamp.

At first, when the bombardment begins, most of the work is performed on the surface of the button, but when a highly conducting photosphere is formed the button is comparatively relieved. The higher the incandescence of the photosphere the more it approaches in conductivity to that of the electrode, and the more, therefore, the solid and the gas form one conducting body. The consequence is that the further is forced the incandescence the more work, comparatively, is performed on the gas, and the less on the electrode. The formation of a powerful photosphere is consequently the very means for protecting the electrode. This protection, of course, is a relative one, and it should not be thought that by pushing the incandescence higher the electrode is actually less deteriorated. Still, theoretically, with extreme frequencies, this result must be reached, but probably at a temperature too high for most of the refractory bodies known. Given, then, an electrode which can withstand to a very high limit the effect of the bombardment and outward strain, it would be safe no matter how much it is forced beyond that limit. In an incandescent lamp quite different considerations apply. There the gas is not at all concerned: the whole of the work is performed on the filament; and the life of the lamp diminishes so rapidly with the increase of the degree of incandescence the economical reasons compel us to work it at a low incandescence. But if an incandescent lamp is operated with currents of very high frequency, the action of the gas cannot be neglected, and the rules for the most economical working must be considerably modified.

In order to bring such a lamp with one or two electrodes to a great perfection, it is necessary to employ impulses of very high frequency. The high frequency secures, among others, two chief advantages, which have a most important bearing upon the economy of the light production. First, the deterioration of the electrode is reduced by reason of the fact that we employ a great many small impacts, instead of a few violent ones, which shatter quickly the structure; secondly, the formation of a large photosphere is facilitated.

In order to reduce the deterioration of the electrode to the minimum, it is desirable that the vibration be harmonic, for any suddenness hastens the process of destruction. An electrode lasts much longer when kept at incandescence by currents, or impulses, obtained from a high-frequency alternator, which rise and fall more or less harmonically, than by impulses obtained from a disruptive discharge coil. In the latter case there is no doubt that most of the damage is done by the fundamental sudden discharges.

One of the elements of loss in such a lamp is the bombardment of the globe. As the potential is very high, the molecules are projected with great speed; they strike the glass, and usually excite a strong phosphorescence. The effect produced is very pretty but for economical reasons it would be perhaps preferable to prevent, or at least reduce to the minimum, the bombardment against the globe, as in such case it is, as a result, not the object to excite phosphorescence, and as some loss of energy results from the bombardment. This loss in the bulb is principally dependent on the potential of the impulses and on the electric density on the surface of the electrode. In employing very high frequencies the loss of energy by the bombardment is greatly reduced, for, first, the potential needed to perform a given amount of work is much smaller; and, secondly, by producing a highly conducting photosphere around the electrode, the same result is obtained as though the electrode were much larger, which is equivalent to a smaller electric density. But be it by the diminution of the maximum potential or of the density, the gain is effected in the same manner, namely, by avoiding violent shocks, which strain the glass much beyond its limit of elasticity. If the frequency could be brought high enough, the loss due to the imperfect elasticity of the glass would be entirely negligible. The loss due to bombardment of the globe may, however, be reduced by using two electrodes instead of one. In such case each of the electrodes may be connected to one of the terminals; or else, if it is preferable to use only one wire, one electrode may be connected to one terminal and the other to the ground or to an insulated body of some surface, as, for instance, a shade on the lamp. In the latter case, unless some judgment is used, one of the electrodes might glow more intensely than the other.

But on the whole I find it preferable when using such high frequencies to employ only one electrode and one connecting wire. I am convinced that the illuminating device of the near future will not require for its operation more than one lead, and, at any rate, it will have no leading-in wire, since the energy required can be as well transmitted through the glass. In experimental bulbs the leading-in wire is most generally used on account of convenience, as in employing condenser coatings in the manner indicated in Fig. 22, for example, there is some difficulty in fitting the parts, but these difficulties would not exist if a great many bulbs were manufactured; otherwise the energy can be conveyed through the glass as well as through a wire, and with these high frequencies the losses are very small. Such illuminating deices will necessarily involve the use of very high potentials, and this, in the eyes of practical men, might be an objectionable feature. Yet, in reality, high potentials are not objectionable—certainly not in the least as far as the safety of the devices is concerned.

There are two ways of rendering an electric appliance safe. One is to use low potentials, the other is to determine the dimensions of the apparatus so that it is safe no matter how high a potential is used. Of the two the latter seems to me the better way, for then the safety is absolute, unaffected by any possible combination of circumstances which might render even a low-potential appliance dangerous to life and property. But the practical conditions require not only the judicious determination of the dimensions of the apparatus; they likewise necessitate the employment of energy of the proper kind. It is easy, for instance, to construct a transformer capable of giving, when operated from an ordinary alternate current machine of low tension, say 50,000 volts, which might be required to light a highly exhausted phosphorescent tube, so that, in spite of the high potential, it is perfectly safe, the shock from it producing no inconvenience. Still, such a transformer would be expensive, and in itself inefficient; and, besides, what energy was obtained from it would not be economically used for the production of light. The economy demands the employment of energy in the form of extremely rapid vibrations. The problem of producing light has been likened to that of maintaining a certain high-pitch note by means of a bell. It should be said a *barely audible* note; and even these words would not express it, so wonderful is the sensitiveness of the eye. We may deliver powerful blows at long intervals, waste a good deal of energy, and still not get what we want; or we may keep up the note by delivering frequent gentle taps, and get nearer to the object sought by the expenditure of mud—l less energy. In the production of light, as far as the illuminating device is concerned, there can be only one rule—that is, to use as high frequencies as can be obtained; but the means for the production and conveyance of impulses of such character impose, at present at least, great limitations. Once it is decided to use very high frequencies, the return wire becomes unnecessary, and all the appliances are simplified. By the use of obvious means the same result is obtained as though the return wire were used. It is sufficient for this purpose to bring in contact with the bulb, or merely in the vicinity of the same, an insulated body of some surface. The surface need, of course, be the smaller, the higher the frequency and potential used, and necessarily, also, the higher the economy of the lamp or other device.

This plan of working has been resorted to on several occasions this evening. So, for instance, when the incandescence of a button was produced by grasping the bulb with the hand, the body of the experimenter merely served to intensify the action. The bulb used was similar to that illustrated in Fig. 19, and the coil was excited to a small potential, not sufficient to bring the button to incandescence when the bulb was hanging from the wire; and incidentally, in order to perform the experiment in a more suitable manner, the button was taken so large that a perceptible time had to elapse before, upon grasping the bulb, it could be rendered incandescent. The contact with the bulb was, of course, quite unnecessary. It is easy, by using a rather large bulb with an exceedingly small electrode, to adjust the conditions so that the latter is brought to bright incandescence by the mere approach of the experimenter within a few feet of the bulb, and that the incandescence subsides upon his receding.

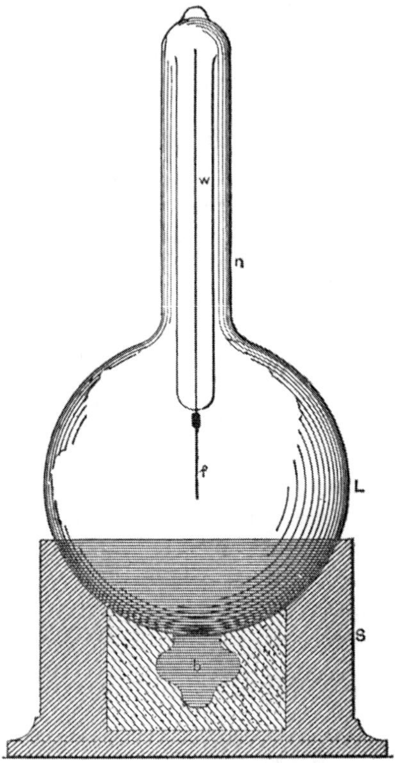

FIG. 24.—BULB WITHOUT LEADING-IN WIRE, SHOWING EFFECT

In another experiment, when phosphorescence was excited, a similar bulb was used. Here again, originally, the potential was not sufficient to excite phosphorescence until the action was intensified—in this case, however, to present a different feature, by touching the socket with a metallic object held in the hand. The electrode in the bulb was a carbon button so large that it could not be brought to incandescence, and thereby spoil the effect produced by phosphorescence.

Again, in another of the early experiments, a bulb was used as illustrated in Fig. 12. In this instance, by touching the bulb with one or two fingers, one or two shadows of the stem inside were projected against the glass, the touch of the finger producing the same result as the application of an external negative electrode under ordinary circumstances.

In all these experiments the action was intensified by augmenting the capacity at the end of the lead connected to the terminal. As a rule, it is not necessary to resort to such means, and would be quite unnecessary with still higher frequencies; but when it is desired, the bulb, or tube, can be easily adapted to the purpose.

In Fig. 24, for example, an experimental bulb *L* is shown, which is provided with a neck *n* on the top for the application of an external tinfoil coating, which may be connected to a body of larger surface. Sum a lamp as illustrated in Fig. 25 may also be lighted by connecting the tinfoil coating on the neck *n* to the terminal, and the leading-in wire *w* to an insulated plate. If the bulb stands in a socket upright, as shown in the cut, a shade of conducting material may be slipped in the neck *n*, and the action thus magnified.

A more perfected arrangement used in some of these bulbs is illustrated in Fig. 26. In this case the construction of the bulb is as shown and described before, where reference was made to Fig. 19. A zinc sheet *Z*, with a tubular extension *T*, is slipped over the metallic socket *S*. The bulb hangs downward from the terminal *t*, the zinc sheet *Z*, performing the double office of intensifier and reflector. The reflector is separated from the terminal *t* by an extension of the insulating plug *P*.

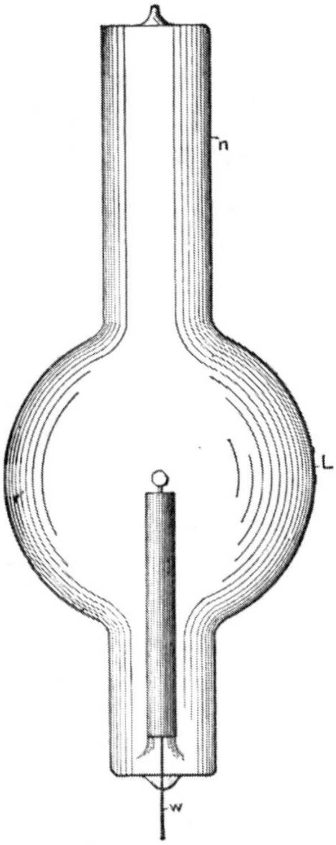

Fig. 25.—Improved Experimental Bulb.

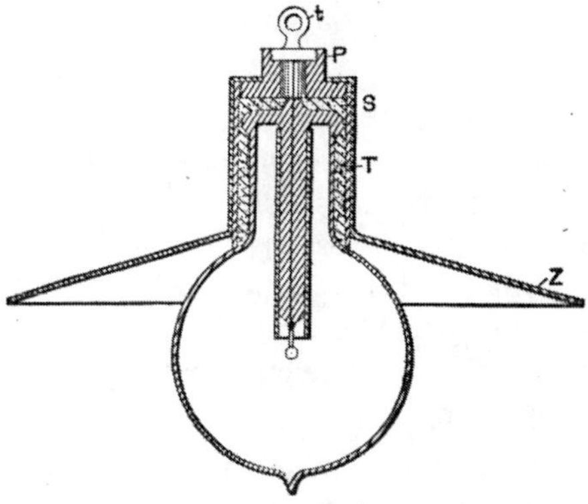

Fig. 26.—Improved Bulb with Intensifying Reflector.

A similar disposition with a phosphorescent tube is illustrated in Fig. 27. The tube *T* is prepared from two short tubes of a different diameter, which are sealed on the ends. On the lower end is placed an outside conducting coating *C*, which connects to the wire *w*. The wire has a hook on the upper end for suspension, and passes through the centre of the inside tube, which is filled with some good and tightly packed insulator. On the outside of the upper end of the tube, *T*, is another conducting coating C_1, upon which is slipped a metallic reflector *Z*, which should be separated by a thick insulation from the end of wire *w*.

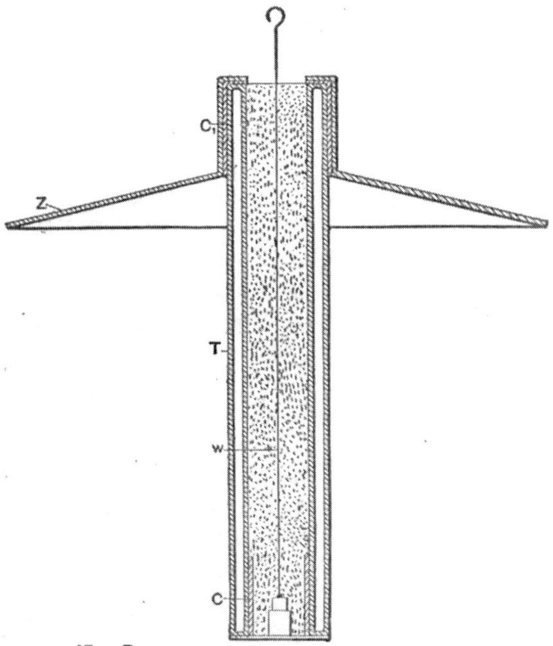

FIG. 27.—PHOSPHORESCENT TUBE WITH INTENSIFYING.

The economical use of such a reflector or intensifier would require that all energy supplied to an air condenser should be recoverable, or, in other words, that there should not be any losses, neither in the gaseous medium nor through its action elsewhere. This is far from being so, but, fortunately, the losses may be reduced to anything desired. A few remarks are necessary on this subject, in order to make the experiences gathered in the course of these investigations perfectly clear.

Suppose a small helix with many well insulated turns, as in experiment Fig. 17, had one of its ends connected to one of the terminals of the induction coil, and the other to a metal plate, or, for the sake of simplicity, a sphere, insulated in space. When the coil is set to work, the potential of the sphere is alternated, and the small helix now behaves as though its free end were connected to the other terminal of the induction coil. If an iron can be held within the small helix it is quickly brought to a high temperature, indicating the passage of a strong current through the helix. How does the insulated sphere act in this case? It can be a condenser, storing and returning the energy supplied to it, or it can be a mere sink of energy, and the conditions of the experiment determine whether it is more one or the other. The sphere being charged to a high potential, it acts inductively upon the surrounding air, or whatever gaseous medium there might be. The molecules, or atoms, which are near the sphere are of course more attracted, and move through a greater distance than the farther ones. When the nearest molecules strike the sphere they are repelled, and collisions occur at all distances within the inductive action of the sphere. It is now clear that, if the potential be steady, but little loss of energy can be caused in this way, for the molecules which are nearest to the sphere, having had an additional charge imparted to them by contact, are not Attracted until they have parted, if not with all, at least with most of the additional charge, which can be accomplished only after a great many collisions. From the fact that with a steady potential there is but little loss in dry air, one must come to such a conclusion. When the potential of the sphere, instead of being steady, is alternating, the conditions are entirely different. In this case a rhythmical bombardment occurs, no matter whether the molecules after coming in contact with the sphere lose the imparted charge or not; what is more, if the charge is not lost, the impacts are only the more violent. Still if the frequency of the impulses be very small, the loss caused hg the impacts and collisions would not be serious unless the potential were excessive. But when extremely high frequencies and more or less high potentials are used, the loss may be very great. The total energy lost per unit of time is proportionate to the product of the number of impacts per second, or the frequency and the energy lost in each impact. But the energy of an impact must be proportionate to the square of the electric density of the sphere, since the charge imparted to the molecule is proportionate to that density. I conclude from this that the total energy lost must be proportionate to the product of the frequency and the square of the electric density; but this law needs experimental confirmation. Assuming the preceding considerations to be true, then, by rapidly alternating the potential of a body immersed in an insulating gaseous medium, any amount of energy may be dissipated into space. Most of that energy then, I believe, is not dissipated in the form of long ether waves, propagated to considerable distance, as is thought most generally, but is consumed—in the case of an insulated sphere, for example—in impact and collisional losses—that is, heat vibrations—on the surface and in the vicinity of the sphere. To reduce the dissipation it is necessary to work with a small electric density the smaller the higher the frequency.

But since, on the assumption before made, the loss is diminished with the square of the density, and since currents of very high frequencies involve considerable waste when transmitted through conductors, it follows that, on the whole, it is better to employ one wire than two. Therefore, if motors, lamps, or devices of any kind are perfected, capable of being advantageously operated by currents of extremely high frequency, economical reasons will make it advisable to use only one wire, especially if the distances are great.

When energy is absorbed in a condenser the same behaves as though its capacity were increased. Absorption always exists more or less, but generally it is small and of no consequence as long as the frequencies are not very great. In using extremely high frequencies, and, necessarily in such case, also high potentials, the absorption—or, what is here meant more particularly by this term, the loss of energy due to the presence of a gaseous medium—is an important factor to be considered, as the energy absorbed it the air condenser may be any fraction of the supplied energy. This would seem to make it very difficult to tell from the measured or computed capacity of an air condenser its actual capacity or vibration period, especially if the condenser is of very small surface and is charged to a very high potential. As many important results are dependent upon the correctness of the estimation of the vibration period, this subject demands the most careful scrutiny of other investigators. To reduce the probable error as much as possible in experiments of the kind alluded to, it is advisable to use spheres or plates of large surface, so as to make the density exceedingly small. Otherwise, when it is practicable, an oil condenser should be used in preference. In oil or other liquid dielectrics there are seemingly no such losses as in gaseous media. It being impossible to exclude entirely the gas in condensers with solid dielectrics, such condensers should be immersed in oil, for economical reasons if nothing else; they can then be strained to the utmost and will remain cool. In Leyden jars the loss due to air is comparatively small, as the tinfoil coatings are large, close together, and the charged surfaces not directly exposed; but when the potentials are very high, the loss may be more or less considerable at, or near, the upper edge of the foil, where the air is principally acted upon. If the jar be immersed in boiled-out oil, it will be capable of performing four times the amount of work which it can for any length of time when used in the ordinary way, and the loss will be inappreciable.

It should not be thought that the loss in heat in an air condenser is necessarily associated with the formation of *visible* streams or brushes. If a small electrode, inclosed in an unexhausted bulb, is connected to one of the terminals of the coil, streams can be seen to issue from the electrode and the air in the bulb is heated; if, instead of a small electrode, a large sphere is inclosed in the bulb, no streams are observed, still the air is heated.

Nor should it be thought that the temperature of an air condenser would give even an approximate idea of the loss in heat incurred, as in such case heat must be given off much more quickly, since there is, in addition to the ordinary radiation, a very active carrying away of heat by independent carriers going on, and since not only the apparatus, but the air at some distance from it is heated in consequence of the collisions which must occur.

Owing to this, in experiments with such a coil, a rise of temperature can be distinctly observed only when the body connected to the coil is very small. But with apparatus on a larger scale, even a body of considerable bulk would be heated, as, for instance, the body of a person; and I think that skilled physicians might make observations of utility in such experiments, which, if the apparatus were judiciously designed, would not present the slightest danger.

A question of some interest, principally to meteorologists, presents itself here. How does the earth behave? The earth is an air condenser, but is it a perfect or a very imperfect one—a mere sink of energy? There can be little doubt that to such small disturbance as might be caused in an experiment the earth behaves as an almost perfect condenser. But it might be different when its charge is set in vibration by some sudden disturbance occurring in the heavens. In such case, as before stated, probably only little of the energy of the vibrations set up would be lost into space in the form of long ether radiations, but most of the energy, I think, would spend itself in molecular impacts and collisions, and pass off into space in the form of short heat, and possibly light, waves. As both the frequency of the vibrations of the charge and the potential are in all probability excessive, the energy converted into heat may be considerable. Since the density must be unevenly distributed, either in consequence of the irregularity of the earth's surface, or on account of the condition of the atmosphere in various places, the effect produced would accordingly vary from place to place. Considerable variations in the temperature and pressure of the atmosphere may in this manner be caused at any point of the surface of the earth. The variations may be gradual or very sudden, according to the nature of the general disturbance, and may produce rain and storms, or locally modify the weather in any way.

From the remarks before made one may see what an important factor of loss the air in the neighborhood of a charged surface becomes when the electric density is great and the frequency of the impulses excessive. But the action as explained implies that the air is insulating—that is, that it is composed of independent carriers immersed in an insulating medium. This is the case only when the air is at something like ordinary or greater, or at extremely small, pressure. When the air is slightly rarefied and conducting, then true conduction losses occur also. In such case, of course, considerable energy may be dissipated into space even with a steady potential, or with impulses of low frequency, if the density is very great.

When the gas is at very low pressure, an electrode is heated more because higher speeds can be reached. If the gas around the electrode is strongly compressed, the displacements, and consequently the speeds, are very small, and the heating is insignificant. But if in such case the frequency could be sufficiently increased, the electrode would be brought to a high temperature as well as if the gas were at very low pressure; in fact, exhausting the bulb is only necessary because we cannot produce (and possibly not convey) currents of the required frequency.

Returning to the subject of electrode lamps, it is obviously of advantage in such a lamp to confine as much as possible the heat to the electrode by preventing the circulation of the gas in the bulb. If a very small bulb be taken, it would confine the heat better than a large one, but it might not be of sufficient capacity to be operated from the coil, or, if so, the glass might get too hot. A simple way to improve in this direction is to employ a globe of the required size, but to place a small bulb, the diameter of which is properly estimated, over the refractory button contained in the globe. This arrangement is illustrated in Fig. 28.

The globe L has in this case a large neck *n*, allowing the small bulb *b* to slip through. Otherwise the construction is the same as shown in Fig. 18, for example. The small bulb is conveniently supported upon the stem *s*, carrying the refractory button *m*. In tube a by several layers of mica *M*, in order to prevent the cracking of the neck by the rapid heating of the aluminium tube upon a sudden turning on of the current. The inside bulb should be as small as possible when it is desired to obtain light only by incandescence of the electrode. If it is desired to produce phosphorescence, the bulb should be larger, else it would be apt to get too hot, and the phosphore-scence would cease. In this arrangement usually only the small bulb shows phosphorescence, as there is practically no bombardment against the outer globe. In some of these bulbs constructed as illustrated in Fig. 28 the small tube was coated with phosphorescent paint, and beautiful effects were obtained. Instead of making the inside bulb large, in order to avoid undue heating, it answers the purpose to make the electrode *m* larger. In this case the bombardment is weakened by reason of the smaller electric density.

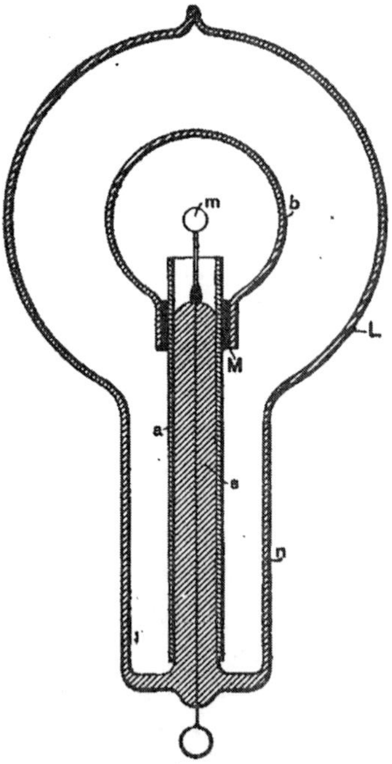

FIG. 28.—LAMP WITH AUXILIARY BULB FOR CONFINING THE ACTION TO THE CENTRE.

Many bulbs were constructed on the plan illustrated in Fig. 29. Here a small bulb *b*, containing the refractory button *m*, upon being exhausted to a very high degree was sealed in a large globe L, which was then moderately exhausted and sealed off. The principal advantage of this construction was that it allowed of reaching extremely high vacua, and, at the same time use a large bulb. It was found, in the course of experiences with bulbs such as illustrated in Fig. 29, that it was well to make the stem *s* near the seal at *c* very thick, and the leading-in wire *w* thin, as it occurred sometimes that the stem at *e* was heated and the bulb was cracked. Often the outer globe L was exhausted only just enough to allow the discharge to pass through, and the space between the bulbs appeared crimson, producing a curious effect. In some cases, when the exhaustion in globe L was very low, and the air good conducting, it was found necessary, in order to bring the button *m* to high incandescence, to place, preferably on the upper part of the neck of the globe, a tinfoil coating which was connected to an insulated body, to the ground, or to the other terminal of the coil, as the highly conducting air weakened the effect somewhat, probably by being acted upon inductively from the wire *w*, where it entered the bulb at *e*. Another difficulty—which, however, is always present when the refractory button is mounted in a very small bulb—existed in the construction illustrated in Fig. 29, namely, the vacuum in the bulb *b* would be impaired in a comparatively short time.

The chief idea in the two last described constructions was to confine the heat to the central portion of the globe by preventing the exchange of air. An advantage is secured, but owing to the heating of the inside bulb and slow evaporation of the glass the vacuum is hard to maintain, even if the construction illustrated in Fig. 28 be chosen, in which both bulbs communicate.

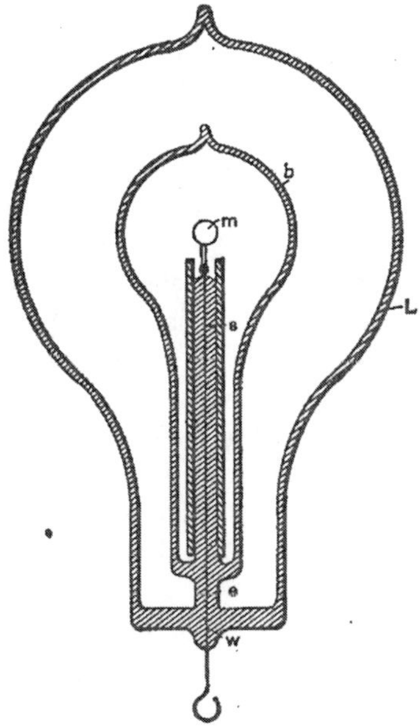

FIG. 29.—LAMP WITH INDEPENDENT AUXILIARY BULB.

But by far the better way—the ideal way—would be to reach sufficiently high frequencies. The higher the frequency the slower would be the exchange of the air, and I think that a frequency may be reached at which there would be no exchange whatever of the air molecules around the terminal. We would then produce a flame in which there would be no carrying away of material, and a queer flame it would be, for it would be rigid! With such high frequencies the inertia of the particles, would come into play. As the brush, or flame, would gain rigidity in virtue of the inertia of the particles, the exchange of the latter would be prevented. This would necessarily occur, for, the number of the impulses being augmented, the potential energy of each would diminish, so that finally only atomic vibrations could be set up, and the motion of translation through measurable space would cease. Thus an ordinary gas burner connected to a source of rapidly alternating potential might have its efficiency augmented to a certain limit, and this for two reasons—because of the additional vibration imparted, and because of a slowing down of the process of carrying off. But the renewal being rendered difficult, and renewal being necessary to maintain the *burner*, a continued increase of the frequency of the impulses, assuming they could be transmitted to and impressed upon the flame, would result in the "extinction" of the latter, meaning by this term only the cessation of the chemical process.

I think, however, that in the case of an electrode immersed in a fluid insulating medium, and surrounded by independent carriers of electric charges, which can be acted upon inductively, a sufficiently high frequency of the impulses would probably result in a gravitation of the gas all around toward the electrode. For this it would be only necessary to assume that the independent bodies are irregularly shaped; they would then turn toward the electrode their side of the greatest electric density, and this would be a position in which the fluid resistance to approach would be smaller than that offered to the receding.

The general opinion, I do not doubt, is that it is out of the question to reach any such frequencies as might—assuming some of the views before expressed to be true produce any of the results which I have pointed out as mere possibilities. This may be so, but in the course of these investigations, from the observation of many phenomena I have gained the conviction that these frequencies would be much lower than one is apt to estimate at first. In a flame we set up light vibrations by causing molecules, of atoms, to collide. But what is the ratio of the frequency of the collisions and that of the vibrations set up? Certainly it must be incomparably smaller than that of the knocks of the bell and the sound vibrations, or that of the discharges and the oscillations of the condenser. We may cause the molecules of the gas to collide by the use of alternate electric impulses of high frequency, and so we may imitate the process in a flame; and from experiments with frequencies which we are now able to obtain, I think that the result is producible with impulses which are transmissible through a conductor.

In connection with thoughts of a similar nature, it appeared to me of great interest to demonstrate the rigidity of a vibrating gaseous column. Although with such low frequencies as, say 10,000 per second, which I was able to obtain without difficulty from a specially constructed alternator, the task looked discouraging at first, I made a series of experiments. The trials with air at ordinary pressure led to no result, but with air moderately rarefied I obtain what I think to be an unmistakable experimental evidence of the property sought for. As a result of this kind might lead able investigators to conclusions of importance I will describe one of the experiments performed.

It is well known that when a tube is slightly exhausted the discharge may be passed through it in the form of a thin luminous thread. When produced with currents of low frequency, obtained from a coil operated as usual, this thread is inert. If a magnet be approached to it, the part near the same is attracted or repelled, according to the direction of the lines of force of the magnet. It occurred to me that if such a thread would be produced with currents of very high frequency, it should be more or less rigid, and as it was visible it could be easily studied. Accordingly I prepared a tube about 1 inch in diameter and 1 metre long, with outside coating at each end. The tube was exhausted to a point at which, by a little working the thread discharge could be obtained. It must be remarked here that the general aspect of the tube, and the degree of exhaustion, are quite different than when ordinary low frequency currents are used. As it was found preferable to work with one terminal, the tube prepared was suspended from the end of a wire connected to the terminal, the tinfoil coating being connected to the wire, and to the lower coating sometimes a small insulated plate was attached. When the thread was formed it extended through the upper part of the tube and lost itself in the lower end. If it possessed rigidity it resembled, not exactly an elastic cord stretched tight between two supports, but a cord suspended from a height with a small weight attached at the end. When the finger or a magnet was approached to the upper end of the luminous thread, it could be brought locally out of position by electrostatic or magnetic action; and when the disturbing object was very quickly removed, an analogous result was produced, as though a suspended cord would be displaced and quickly released near the point of suspension. In doing this the luminous thread was set in vibration, and two very sharply marked nodes, and a third indistinct one, were formed. The vibration, once set up, continued for fully eight minutes, dying gradually out. The speed of the vibration often varied perceptibly, and it could be observed that the electrostatic attraction of the glass affected the vibrating thread; but it was clear that the electrostatic action was not the cause of the vibration, for the thread was most generally stationary, and could always be set in vibration by passing the finger quickly near the upper part of the tube. With a magnet the thread could be split in two and both parts vibrated. By approaching the hand to the lower coating of the tube, or insulated plate if attached, the vibration was quickened; also, as far as I could see, by raising the potential of frequency. Thus, either increasing the frequency or passing a stronger discharge of the same frequency corresponded to a tightening of the cord. I did not obtain any experimental evidence with condenser discharges. A luminous band excited in a bulb by repeated discharges of a Leyden jar must possess rigidity, and if deformed and suddenly released should vibrate. But probably the amount of vibrating matter is so small that in spite of the extreme speed the inertia cannot prominently assert itself. Besides, the observation in such a case is rendered extremely difficult on account of the fundamental vibration.

The demonstration of the fact—which still needs better experimental confirmation—that a vibrating gaseous column possesses rigidity, might greatly modify the views of thinkers. When with low frequencies and insignificant potentials indications of that property may be noted, how must a gaseous medium behave under the influence of enormous electrostatic stresses which may be active in the interstellar space, and which may alternate with inconceivable rapidity! The existence of such an electrostatic, rhythmically throbbing force—of a vibrating electrostatic field—would show a possible way how solids might have formed from the ultra-gaseous uterus, and how transverse and all kinds of vibrations may be transmitted through a gaseous medium filling all space. Then, ether might be a true fluid, devoid of rigidity, and at rest, it being merely necessary as a connecting link to enable interaction. What determines the rigidity of a body? It must be the speed and the amount of moving matter. In a gas the speed may be considerable, but the density is exceedingly small; in a liquid the speed would be likely to be small, though the density may be considerable; and in both cases the inertia resistance offered to displacement is practically *nil.* But place a gaseous (or liquid) column in an intense, rapidly alternating electrostatic field, set the particles vibrating with enormous speeds, then the inertia resistance asserts itself. A body might move with more or less freedom through the vibrating mass, but as a whole it would be rigid.

There is a subject which I must mention in connection with these experiments: it is that of high vacua. This is a subject the study of which is not only interesting, but useful, for it may lead to results of great practical importance. In commercial apparatus such as incandescent lamps, operated from ordinary systems of distribution, a much higher vacuum than obtained at present would not secure a very great advantage. In such a case the work is performed on the filament and the gas is little concerned; the improvement, therefore, would be but trifling. But when we begin to use very high frequencies and potentials, the action of the gas becomes all important, and the degree of exhaustion materially modifies the results. As long as ordinary coils, even very large ones, were used, the study of the subject was limited, because just at a point when it became most interesting it had to be interrupted on account of the "non-striking" vacuum being reached. But presently we are able to obtain from a small disruptive discharge coil potentials much higher than even the largest coil was capable of giving, and, what is more, we can make the potential alternate with great rapidity. Both of these results enable us now to pass a luminous discharge through almost any vacua obtainable, and the field of our investigations is greatly extended. Think we as we may, of all the possible directions to develop a practical illuminant, the line of high vacua seems to be the most promising at present. But to reach extreme vacua the appliances must be much mote improved, and ultimate perfection will not be attained until we shall have discarded the mechanical and perfected an *electrical* vacuum pump. Molecules and atoms can be thrown out of a bulb under the action of an enormous potential: *this* will be the principle of the vacuum pump of the future. For the present, we must secure the best results we can with mechanical appliances. In this respect, it might not be out of the way to say a few words about the method of, and apparatus for, producing excessively high degrees of exhaustion of which I have availed myself in the course of these investigations. It is very probable that other experimenters have used similar arrangements; but as it is possible that there may be an item of interest in their description, a few remarks, which will render this investigation more complete, might be permitted.

The apparatus is illustrated in a drawing shown in Fig. 30. S represents a Sprengel pump, which has been specially constructed to better suit the work required. The stopcock which is usually employed has been omitted, and instead of it a hollow stopper has been fitted in the neck of the reservoir R. This stopper has a small hole *h*, through which the mercury descends; the size of the outlet *o* being properly determined with respect to the section of the

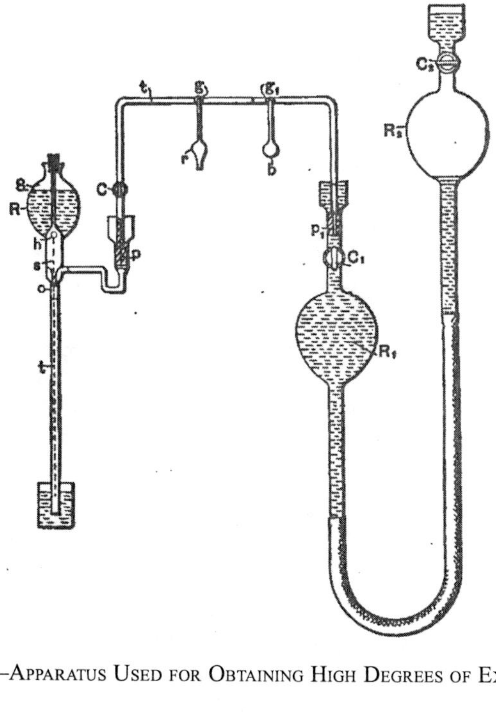

FIG. 30.—APPARATUS USED FOR OBTAINING HIGH DEGREES OF EXHAUSTION.

fall tube *t*, which is sealed to the reservoir instead of being connected to it in the usual manner. This arrangement overcomes the imperfections and troubles, which often arise from the use of the stopcock on the reservoir and the connection of the latter with the fall tube.

The pump is connected through a **U**-shaped tube *t* to a very large reservoir R_1. Especial care was taken in fitting the grinding surfaces of the stoppers *p* and p_1 and both of these and the mercury caps above them were made exceptionally long. After the **U**-shaped tube was fitted and put in place, it was heated, so as to soften and take off the strain resulting from imperfect fitting. The **U**-shaped tube was provided with a stopcock C, and two ground connections *g* and g_1—one for a small bulb *b*, usually containing caustic potash, and the other for the receiver *r*, to be exhausted.

The reservoir R_1 was connected by means of a rubber tube to a slightly larger reservoir R_2, each of the two reservoirs being provided with a stopcock C_1 and C_2 respectively. The reservoir R_2 could be raised and lowered by a wheel and rack, and the range of its motion was so determined that when it was filled with mercury and the stopcock *C*, closed, so as to form a Torricellian vacuum in it when raised, it could be lifted so high that the mercury in reservoir R_1 would stand a little above stopcock C_1: and when this stopcock was closed and the reservoir R_2 descended, so as to form a Torricellian vacuum in reservoir R_1, it could be lowered so far as to completely empty the latter, the mercury filling the reservoir R_2 up to a little above stopcock C_2.

The capacity of the pump and of the connections was taken as small as possible relatively to the volume of reservoir, R_1, since, of course, the degree of exhaustion depended upon the ratio of these quantities.

With this apparatus I combined the usual means indicated by former experiments for the production of very high vacua. In most of the experiments it was convenient to use caustic potash. I may venture to say, in regard to its use, that much time is saved and a more perfect action of the pump insured by fusing and boiling the potash *w* soon as, or even before, the pump settles down. If this course is not followed the sticks, as ordinarily employed, may give moisture off at a certain very slow rate, and the pump may work for many hours without reaching a very high vacuum. The potash was heated either by a spirit lamp or by passing a discharge through it, or by passing a current through a wire contained in it. The advantage in the latter case was that the heating could be more rapidly repeated.

Generally the process of exhaustion was the following:—at the start, the stopcocks *C* and C_1 being open, and all other connections closed, the reservoir R_2 was raised so far that the mercury filled the reservoir R_1 and a part: of the narrow connecting **U**-shaped tube. When the pump was set to work, the mercury would, of course, quickly rise in the tube, and reservoir R_2 was lowered, the experimenter keeping the mercury at about the same level. The reservoir R_2

was balanced by a long spring which facilitated the operation, and the friction of the parts was generally sufficient to keep it almost in any position. When the Sprengel pump had done its work, the reservoir R_2 was further lowered and the mercury descended in R_1 and filled R_2, whereupon stopcock C_2 was closed. The air adhering to the walls of R, and that absorbed by the mercury was carried off, and to free the mercury of all air the reservoir R_2 was for a long time worked up and down. During this process some air, which would gather below stopcock C_2, was expelled from R_2 by lowering it far enough and opening the stopcock, closing the latter again before raising the reservoir. When all the air had been expelled from the mercury, and no air would gather in R_2 when it was lowered, the caustic potash was resorted to. The reservoir R_2 was now again raised until the mercury in R_1 stood above stopcock C_1. The caustic potash was fused and boiled, and the moisture partly carried off by the pump and partly re-absorbed; and this process of heating and cooling was repeated many times, and each time, upon the moisture being absorbed or carried off, the reservoir R_2 was for a long time raised and lowered. In this manner all the moisture was carried off from the mercury, and both the reservoirs were in proper condition to be used. The reservoir R_2 was then again raised to the top, and the pump was kept working for a long time. When the highest vacuum obtainable with the pump had been reached the potash bulb was usually wrapped with cotton which was sprinkled with ether so as to keep the potash at a very low temperature, then the reservoir R_2 was lowered, and again reservoir R_1 being emptied the receiver r was quickly sealed up.

When a new bulb was put on, the mercury was always raised above stopcock C_1, which was closed, so as to always keep the mercury and both the reservoirs in fine condition, and the mercury was never withdrawn from R_1 except when the pump had reached the highest degree of exhaustion. It is necessary to observe this rule if it is desired to use the apparatus to advantage.

By means of this arrangement I was able to proceed very quickly, and when the apparatus was in perfect order it was possible to reach the phosphorescent stage in a small bulb in less than fifteen minutes, which is certainly very quick work for a small laboratory arrangement requiring all in all about 100 pounds of mercury. With ordinary small bulbs the ratio of the capacity of the pump, receiver, and connections, and that of reservoir R was about 1 to 20, and the degrees of exhaustion reached were necessarily very high, though I am unable to make a precise and reliable statement how far the exhaustion was carried.

What impresses the investigator most in the course of these experiences is the behavior of gases when subjected to great rapidly alternating electrostatic stresses. But he must remain in doubt as to whether the effects observed are due wholly to the molecules, or atoms, of the gas which chemical analysis discloses to us, or whether there enters into play another medium of a gaseous nature, comprising atoms, or molecules, immersed in a fluid pervading the space. Such a medium, surely must exist, and I am convinced that, for instance, even if air were absent, the surface and neighborhood of a body in space would be heated by rapidly alternating the potential of the body; but no such heating of the surface or neighborhood could occur if all free atoms were removed and only a homogeneous, incompressible, and elastic fluid—such as ether is supposed to be—would remain, for then there would be no impacts, no collisions. In such a case, as far as the body itself is concerned, only frictional losses in the inside could occur.

It is a striking fact that the discharge through a gas is established with ever increasing freedom as the frequency of the impulses is augmented. It behaves in this respect quite contrarily to a metallic conductor. In the latter the impedance enters prominently into play as the frequency is increased, but the gas acts much as a series of condensers would: the facility with which the discharge passes through seems to depend on the rate of change of potential. If it act so, then in a vacuum tube even of great length, and no matter how strong the current, self-induction could not assert itself: to any appreciable degree. We have, then, as far as we can now see, in the gas a conductor which is capable of transmitting electric impulses of any frequency which we may be able to produce. Could the frequency be brought high enough, then a queer system of electric distribution, which would be likely to interest gas companies, might be realized : metal pipes filled with gas—the metal being the insulator, the gas the conductor—supplying phosphorescent bulbs, or perhaps devices as yet uninvented. It is certainly possible to take a hollow core of copper, rarefy the gas in the same, and by passing impulses of sufficiently high frequency through a circuit around it, bring the gas inside to a high degree of incandescence; but as to the nature of the forces there would be considerable uncertainty, for it would be doubtful whether with such impulses the copper core would act as a static screen. Such paradoxes and apparent impossibilities we encounter at every step in this line of work, and therein lies, to a great extent, the charm of the study.

I have here a short and wide tube which is exhausted to a high degree and covered with a substantial coating of bronze, the coating allowing barely the light to shine through. A metallic clasp, with a hook for suspending the tube, is fastened around the middle portion of the latter, the clasp being in contact with the bronze coating. I now want to light the gas inside by suspending the tube on a wire connected to the coil. Any one who would try the experiment for the first time, not having any previous experience, would probably take care to be quite alone when making the trial, for fear that he might become the joke of his assistants. Still, the bulb lights in spite of the metal coating, and the light can be distinctly perceived through the latter. A long tube covered with aluminium bronze lights when held in one hand—the other touching the terminal of the coil—quite powerfully. It might be objected that the coatings arc not sufficiently conducting; still, even if they were highly resistant, they ought to screen the gas. They certainly screen it perfectly in a condition of rest, but not by far perfectly when the charge is surging in the coating. But the loss of energy which occurs within the tube, notwithstanding the screen, is occasioned principally by the presence of the gas. Were we to take a large hollow metallic sphere and fill it with a perfect incompressible fluid dielectric, there would be no loss inside of the sphere, and consequently the inside might be considered as perfectly screened, though the potential be very rapidly alternating. Even were the sphere filled with oil, the loss would be incomparably smaller than when the fluid is replaced by a gas, for in the latter case the force produces displacements; that means impact and collisions in the inside.

No matter what the pressure of the gas may be, it becomes an important factor in the bearing of a conductor when the electric density is great and the frequency very high. That in the heating of conductors by lightning discharges air is an element of great importance, is almost as certain as an experimental fact. I may illustrate the action of the air by the following experiment: I take a short tube which is exhausted to a moderate degree and has a platinum wire running through the middle from one end to the other. I pass a steady or low frequency current through the wire, and it is heated uniformly in all parts. The heating here is due to conduction, or frictional losses, and the gas around the wire has—as far as we can see—no function to perform. But now let me pass sudden discharges, or a high frequency current, through the wire. Again the wire is heated, this time principally on the ends and least in the middle portion; and if the frequency of the impulses, or the rate of change, is high enough, the wire might as well be cut in the middle as not, for practically all the heating is due to the rarefied gas: Here the gas might only act as a conductor of no impedance diverting the current from the wire as the impedance of the latter is enormously increased, and merely heating the ends of the wire by reason of their resistance to the passage of the discharge. But it is not at all necessary that the gas in the tube should be conducting; it might be at an extremely low pressure, still the ends of the wire would be heated—as, however, is ascertained by experience -only the two ends would in such case not be electrically connected through the gaseous medium. Now what with these frequencies and potentials occurs in an exhausted tube occurs in the lightning discharges at ordinary pressure. We only need to remember one of the facts arrived at in the course of these investigations, namely, that to impulses of very high frequency the gas at ordinary pressure behaves much in the same manner as though it were at moderately low pressure. I think that in lightning discharges frequently wircs or conducting objects are volatilized merely because air is present, and that, were the conductor immersed in an insulating liquid, it would be safe, for then the energy would have to spend itself somewhere else. From the behavior of gases to sudden impulses of high potential I am led to conclude that there can be no surer way of diverting a lightning discharge than by affording it a passage through a volume of gas, if such a thing can be done in a practical manner.

There are two more features upon which I think it necessary to dwell in connection with these experiments—the "radiant state" and the non-striking vacuum."

Any one who has studied Crookes work must have received the impression that the ''radiant state" is a property of the gas inseparably connected with an extremely high degree of exhaustion. But it should be remembered that the phenomena observed in an exhausted vessel are limited to the character and capacity of the apparatus which is made use of. I think that in a bulb a molecule, or atom, does not precisely move in a straight line because it meets no obstacle, but because the velocity imparted to it is sufficient to propel it in a sensibly straight line. The mean free path is one thing, but the velocity—the energy

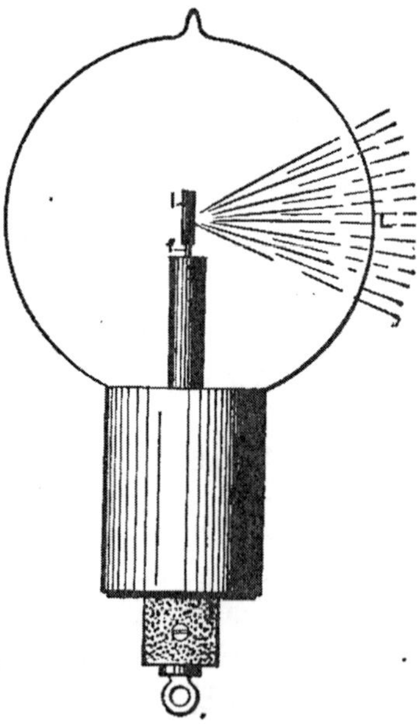

FIG. 31.—BULB SHOWING RADIANT LIME STREAM AT LOW EXHAUSTION.

associated with the moving body—is another, and under ordinary circumstances I believe that it is mere question of potential or speed. A disruptive discharge coil, when the potential is pushed very far, excites phosphorescence and projects shadows, at comparatively low degrees of exhaustion. In a lightning discharge, matter moves in straight lines at ordinary pressure when the mean free path is exceedingly small, and frequently images of wires or other metallic objects have been produced by the particles thrown off in straight lines.

I have prepared a bulb to illustrate by an experiment the correctness of these assertions. In a globe L (Fig. 31), I have mounted upon a lamp filaments of a piece of lime *l*. The lamp filament is connected with a wire which leads into the bulb, and the general construction of the latter is as indicated in Fig. 19, before described. The bulb being suspended from a wire connected to the terminal of the coil, and the latter being set to work, the lime piece *l* and the projecting parts of the filament *f* are bombarded. The degree of exhaustion is just such that with the potential the coil is capable of giving phosphorescence of the glass is produced, but disappears as soon as the vacuum is impaired. The lime containing moisture, and moisture being given off as soon as heating occurs, the phosphorescence lasts only for a few moments. When the lime has been sufficiently heated, enough moisture has been given off to impair materially the vacuum of the bulb. As the bombardment goes on, one point of the lime piece is more heated than other points, and the results is that finally practically all the discharge passes through that point which is intensely heated, and a white stream of lime particles (Fig. 31) then breaks forth from that point. This stream is composed of "radiant" matter, yet the degree of exhaustion is low. But the particles move in straight lines because the velocity imparted to them is great, and this is due to three causes—to the great electric density, the high temperature of the small point, and the fact that the particles of the lime are easily torn and thrown off—far more easily than those of carbon. With frequencies such as we are able to obtain, the particles are bodily thrown off and projected to a considerable distance, but with sufficiently high frequencies no such thing would occur: in such case only a stress would spread or a vibration would be propagated through the bulb. It would be out of the question to reach any such frequency on the assumption that the atoms move with the speed of light; but I believe that such a thing is impossible; for this an enormous potential would be required. With potentials which we are able to obtain, even with a disruptive discharge coil, the speed must be quite insignificant.

As to the "non-striking vacuum," the point to be noted is that it can occur only with low frequency impulses, and it is necessitated by the impossibility of carrying off enough energy with such impulses in high vacuum since the few atoms which are around the terminal upon coming in contact with the same are repelled and kept at a distance for a comparatively long period of time, and not enough work can be performed to render the effect perceptible to the eye. If the difference of potential between the terminals is raised, the dielectric breaks down. But with very high frequency impulses there is no necessity for such breaking down, since any amount of work can be performed by continually agitating the atoms in the exhausted vessel, provided the frequency is high enough. It is easy to reach—even with frequencies obtained from an alternator as here used—a stage at which the discharge does not pass between two electrodes in a narrow tube, each of these being connected to one of the terminals of the coil, but it is difficult to reach a point at which a luminous discharge would not occur around each electrode.

A thought which naturally presents itself in connection with high frequency currents, is to make use of their powerful electro-dynamic inductive action to produce light effects in a sealed glass globe. The leading-in wire is one of the defects of the present incandescent lamp, and if no other improvement were made, that imperfection at least should be done away with. Following this thought, I have carried on experiments in various directions, of which some were indicated in my former paper. I may here mention one or two more lines of experiment which have been followed up.

Many bulbs were constructed as shown in Fig. 32 and Fig. 33.

In Fig. 32 a wide tube *T* was sealed to a smaller W-shaped tube U, of phosphorescent glass. In the tube *T* was placed a coil *C* of aluminium wire, the ends of which were provided with small spheres *t* and t_1 of aluminium, and reached into the U tube. The tube *T* was slipped into a socket containing a primary coil through which usually the discharges of Leyden jars were directed, and the rarefied gas in the small **U** tube was excited to strong luminosity by the high-tension currents induced in the coil *C*. When Leyden

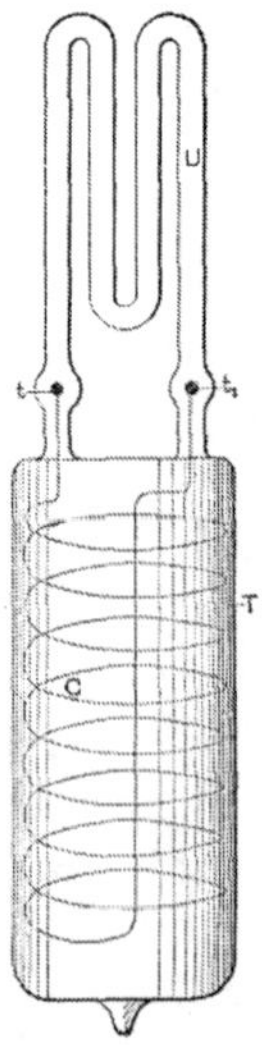

FIG. 32.—ELECTRO-DYNAMIC INDUCTION TUBE.

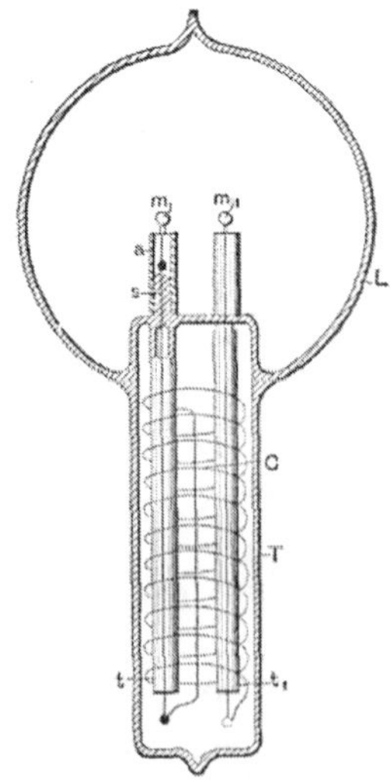

FIG. 33—ELECTRO-DYNAMIC INDUCTION LAMP.

jar discharges were used to induce currents in the coil C, it was found necessary to pack the tube T tightly with insulating powder, as a discharge would occur frequently between the turns of the coil, especially when the primary was thick and the air gap, through which the jars discharged, large, and no little trouble was experienced in this way.

In Fig. 33 is illustrated another form of the bulb constructed. In this case a tube T is sealed to a globe L. The tube contains a coil C, the ends of which pass through two small glass tubes t and t_1, which are sealed to the tube T. Two refractory buttons m and m_1 are mounted on lamp filaments which are fastened to the ends of the wires passing through the glass tubes t and t_1. Generally in bulbs made on this plan the globe L communicated with the tube T. For this purpose the ends of the small tubes t and t_1 were just a trifle heated in the burner, merely to hold the wires, but not to interfere with the communication. The tube T, with the small tubes, wires through the same, and the refractory buttons m and m_1 was first prepared, and then sealed to globe L, whereupon the coil C was slipped in and the connections made to its ends. The tube was then packed with insulating powder, jamming the latter as tight as possible up to very nearly the end, then it was closed and only a small hole left through which the remainder of the powder was introduced, and finally the end of the tube was closed. Usually in bulbs constructed as shown in Fig. 33 an aluminium tube a was fastened to the upper end s of each of the tubes t and t_1, in order to protect that end against the heat. The buttons m and m_1 could be brought to any degree of incandescence by passing the discharges of Leyden jars around the coil C. In such bulbs with two buttons a very curious effect is produced by the formation of the shadows of each of the two buttons.

Another line of experiment, which has been assiduously followed, was to induce by electro-dynamic induction a current or luminous discharge in an exhausted tube or bulb. This matter has received such able treatment at the hands of Prof. J. J. Thomson that I could add but little to what he has made known, even had I made it the special subject of this lecture. Still, since experiences in this line have gradually led me to the present views and results, a few words must be devoted here to this subject.

It has occurred, no doubt, to many that as a vacuum tube is made longer the electromotive force per unit length of the tube, necessary to pass a luminous discharge through the latter, gets continually smaller; therefore, if the exhausted tube be made long enough, even with low frequencies a luminous discharge could be induced in such a tube closed upon itself. Such a tube might be placed around a hall or on a ceiling, and at once a simple appliance capable of giving considerable light would be obtained. But this would be an appliance hard to manufacture and extremely unmanageable. It would not do to make the tube up of small lengths, because there would be with ordinary frequencies considerable loss in the coatings, and besides, if coatings were used, it would be better to supply the current directly to the tube by connecting the coatings to a transformer. But even if all objections of such nature were removed, still, with low frequencies the light conversion itself would be inefficient, as I have before stated. In using extremely high frequencies the length of the secondary—in other words, the site of the vessel—can be reduced as far as desired, and the efficiency of the light conversion is increased; provided that means are invented for efficiently obtaining such high frequencies. Thus one is led, from theoretical and practical considerations, to the use of high frequencies, and this means high electromotive forces and small currents in the primary. When he works with condenser charges—and they are the only means up to the present known for reaching these extreme frequencies—one gets to electromotive forces of several thousands of volts per turn of the primary. He cannot multiply the electro-dynamic inductive effect by taking more turns in the primary, for he arrives at the conclusion that the best way is to work with one single turn—though we must sometimes depart from this rule—and we must get along with whatever inductive effect we can obtain with one turn. But before he has long experimented with the extreme frequencies required to set up in a small bulb an electromotive force of several thousands of volts he realizes the great importance of electrostatic effects, and these effects grow relatively to the electro-dynamic in significance as the frequency is increased.

Now, if anything is desirable in this case, it is to increase the frequency, and this would make it still worse for the electro-dynamic effects. On the other hand, it is easy to exalt the electrostatic action as far as one likes by taking more turns on the secondary, or combining self-induction and capacity to raise the potential. It should also be remembered that, in reducing the current to the smallest value and increasing the potential, the electric impulses of high frequency can be more easily transmitted through a conductor.

These and similar thoughts determined me to devote more attention to the electrostatic phenomena, and to endeavor to produce potentials as high as possible, and alternating as fast as they could be made to alternate. I then found that I could excite vacuum tubes at considerable distance from a conductor connected to a properly constructed coil, and that I could, by converting the oscillatory current of a condenser to a higher potential, establish electrostatic alternating fields which acted through the whole extent of a room, lighting up a tube no matter where it was held in space. I thought I recognized that I had made a step in advance, and I have persevered in this line; but I wish to say that I share with all lovers of science and progress the one and only desire—to reach a result of utility to men in any direction to which thought or experiment may lead me. I think that this departure is the right one, for I cannot see, from the observation of the phenomena which manifest themselves as the frequency is increased, what there would remain to act between two circuits conveying, for instance, impulses of several hundred millions per second, except electrostatic forces. Even with such stifling frequencies the energy would be practically all potential, and my conviction has grown strong that, to whatever kind of motion light may be due, it is produced by tremendous electrostatic stresses vibrating with extreme rapidity.

Of all these phenomena observed with currents, or electric impulses, of high frequency, the most fascinating for an audience are certainly those which are noted in an electrostatic field acting through considerable distance, and the best an unskilled lecturer can do is to begin and finish with the exhibition of these singular effects. I take a tube in the hand and move it about, and it is lighted wherever I may hold it; throughout space the invisible forces act. But I may take another tube and it might not light, the vacuum being very high. I excite it by means of a disruptive discharge coil, and now it will light in the electrostatic field. I may put it away for a few weeks or months, still it retains the faculty of being excited. What change have I produced in the tube in the act of exciting it? If a motion imparted to the atoms, it is difficult to perceive how it can persist so long without being arrested by frictional losses; and if a strain exerted in the dielectric, such as a simple electrification would produce, it is easy to see how it may persist indefinitely but very difficult to understand why such a condition should aid the excitation when we have to deal with potentials which are rapidly alternating.

Since I have exhibited these phenomena for the first time, I have obtained some other interesting effects. For instance, I have produced the incandescence of a button, filament, or wire enclosed in a tube. To get to this result it was necessary to economize the energy which is obtained from the field and direct most of it on the small body to be rendered incandescent. At the beginning the task appeared difficult, but the experiences gathered permitted me to teach the result easily. In Fig. 34 and Fig. 35 two such tubes are illustrated which are prepared for the occasion. In Fig. 34 a short tube T_1, sealed to another long tube T, is provided with a stem s, with a platinum wire sealed in the latter. A very thin lamp filament l is fastened to this wire, and connection to the outside is made through a thin copper wire w. The tube is provided with outside and inside coatings, C and C_1 respectively, and is filled as far as the coatings reach with conducting, and the space above with insulating powder. These coatings are merely used to enable me to perform two experiments with the tube—namely, to produce the effect desired either by direct connection of the body of the experimenter or of another body to the wire w, or by acting inductively through the glass. The stem s is provided with an aluminium tube a for purposes before explained, and only a small part of the filament reaches out of this tube. By holding the tube T_1 anywhere in the electrostatic field the filament is rendered incandescent.

A more interesting piece of apparatus is illustrated in Fig. 35. The construction is the same as before, only instead of the lamp filament a small platinum wire p, sealed in a stem s, and bent above it in a circle, is connected

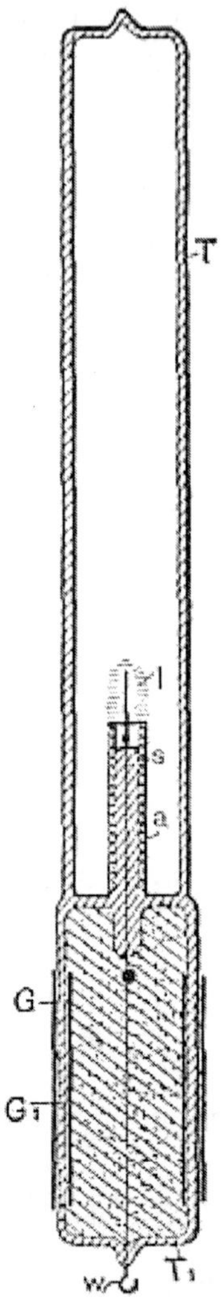

FIG. 34.—TUBE WITH FILAMENT RENDERED INCANDESCENT IN AN ELECTRO STATIC FIELD.

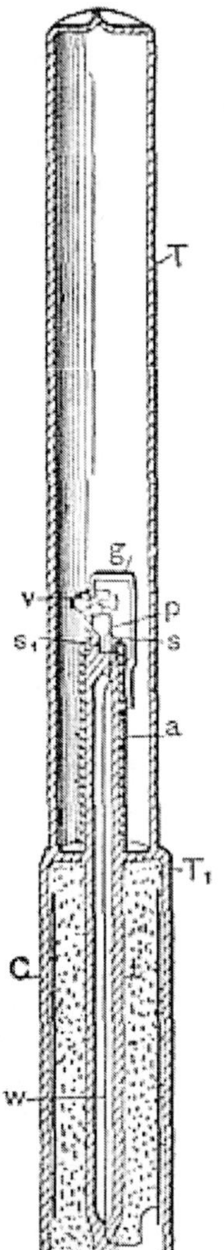

FIG. 35.—CROOKES' EXPERIMENT IN ELECTROSTATIC FIELD.

to the copper wire *w*, which is joined to an inside coating *C*. A small stem s_1 is provided with a needle, on the point of which is arranged to rotate very freely a very light fan of mica *v*. To prevent the fan from falling out, a thin stem of glass *g* is bent properly and fastened to the aluminium tube. When the glass tube is held anywhere in the electrostatic field the platinum wire becomes incandescent, and the mica vanes are rotated very fast.

Intense phosphorescence may be excited in a bulb by merely connecting it to a plate within the field, and the plate need not be any larger than an ordinary lamp shade. The phosphorescence excited with these currents is incomparably more powerful than with ordinary apparatus. A small phosphorescent bulb, when attached to a wire connected to a coil, emits sufficient light to allow reading ordinary print at a distance of five to six paces. It was of interest to see how some of the phosphorescent bulbs of Professor Crookes would behave with these currents, and he has had the kindness to lend me a few for the occasion. The effects produced are magnificent, especially by the sulphide of calcium and sulphide of zinc. From the disruptive discharge coil they glow intensely merely by holding them in the hand and connecting the body to the terminal of the coil.

To whatever results investigations of this kind may lead, their chief interest lies for the present in the possibilities they offer for the production of an efficient illuminating device. In no branch of electric industry is an advance more desired than in the manufacture of light. Every thinker, when considering the barbarous methods employed, the deplorable losses incurred in our best systems of light production, must have asked himself, What is likely to be the light of the future? Is it to be an incandescent solid, as in the present lamp, or an incandescent gas, or a phosphorescent body, or something like a burner, but incomparably more efficient?

There is little chance to perfect a gas burner; not, perhaps, because human ingenuity has been bent upon that problem for centuries without a radical departure having been made—though this argument is not devoid of force—but because in a burner the higher vibrations can never be reached except by passing through all the low ones. For how is a flame produced unless by a fall of lifted weights? Such process cannot be maintained without renewal, and renewal is repeated passing from low to high vibrations. One way only seems to be open to improve a burner, and that is by trying to reach higher degrees of incandescence. Higher incandescence is equivalent to a quicker vibration; that means more light from the same material, and that, again, means more economy. In this direction some improvements have been made, but the progress is hampered by many limitations. Discarding, then, the burner, there remain the three ways first mentioned, which are essentially electrical.

Suppose the light of the immediate future to be a solid rendered incandescent by electricity. Would it not seem that it is better to employ a small button than a frail filament? From many considerations it certainly must be concluded that a button is capable of a higher economy, assuming, of course, the difficulties connected with the operation of such a lamp to be effectively overcome. But to light such a lamp we require a high potential; and to get this economically we must use high frequencies.

Such considerations apply even more to the production of light by the incandescence of a gas, or by phosphorescence. In all cases we require high frequencies and high potentials. These thoughts occurred to me a long time ago.

Incidentally we gain, by the use of very high frequencies, many advantages, such as a higher economy in the light production, the possibility of working with one lead, the possibility of doing away with the leading-in wire, etc.

The question is, how far can we go with frequencies? Ordinary conductors rapidly lose the facility of transmitting electric impulses when the frequency is greatly increased. Assume the means for the production of impulses of very great frequency brought to the utmost perfection, every one will naturally ask how to transmit them when the necessity arises. In transmitting such impulses through conductors we must remember that we have to deal with *pressure* and *flow*, in the ordinary interpretation of these terms. Let the pressure increase to an enormous value, and let the flow correspondingly diminish, then such impulses—variations merely of pressure, as it were—can no doubt be transmitted through a wire even if their frequency be many hundreds of millions per second. It would, of course, be out of question to transmit such impulses through a wire immersed in a gaseous medium, even if the wire were provided with a thick and excellent insulation for most of the energy would be lost in molecular bombardment and consequent heating. The end of the wire connected to the source would be heated, and the remote end would receive but a trifling part of the energy supplied. The prime necessity, then, if such electric impulses are to be used, is to find means to reduce as much as possible the dissipation.

The first thought is, employ the thinnest possible wire surrounded by the thickest practicable insulation. The next thought is to employ electrostatic screens. The insulation of the wire may be covered with a thin conducting coating and the latter connected to the ground. But this would not do, as then all the energy would pass through the conducting coating to the ground and nothing would get to the end of the wire. If a ground connection is made it can only be made through a conductor offering an enormous impedance, or through a condenser of extremely small capacity. This, however, does not do away with other difficulties.

If the wave length of the impulses is much smaller than the length of the wire, then corresponding short waves will be sent up in the conducting coating, and it will be more or less the same as though the coating were directly connected to earth. It is therefore necessary to cut up the coating in sections much shorter than the wave length. Such an arrangement does not still afford a perfect screen, but it is ten thousand times better than none. I think it preferable to cut up the conducting coating in small sections, even if the current waves be much longer than the coating.

If a wire were provided with a perfect electrostatic screen, it would be the same as though all objects were removed from it at infinite distance. The capacity would then be reduced to the capacity of the wire itself, which would be very small. It would then be possible to send over the wire current vibrations of very high frequencies at enormous distance without affecting greatly the character of the vibrations. A perfect screen is of course out of the question, but I believe that with a screen such as I have just described telephony could be rendered practicable across the Atlantic. According to my ideas, the gutta-percha covered wire should be provided with a third conducting coating subdivided in sections. On the top of this should be again placed a layer of gutta-percha and other insulation, and on the top of the whole the armor. But such cables will not be constructed, for ere long intelligence—transmitted without wires will throb through the earth like a pulse through a living organism. The wonder is that, with the present state of knowledge and the experiences gained, no attempt is being made to disturb the electrostatic or magnetic condition of the earth, and transmit, if nothing else, intelligence.

It has been my chief aim in presenting these results to point out phenomena or features of novelty, and to advance ideas which I am hopeful will serve as starting points of new departures. It has been my chief desire this evening to entertain you with some novel experiments. Your applause, so frequently and generously accorded has told me that I have succeeded.

In conclusion, let me thank you most heartily for your kindness and attention, and assure you that the honor I have had in addressing such a distinguished audience, the pleasure I have had in presenting these results to a gathering of so many able men and among them also some of those in whose work for many years past I have found enlightenment and constant pleasure—I shall never forget.